Murder On Account

Published by Implode Publishing Ltd
© Implode Publishing Ltd 2019

Chapter 1

"Is this R.K. Investigations?" The young delivery guy had a mouthful of gum and a face full of spots. "I've got a parcel for Roy King."

"That's us." Sheila was on her feet before my brain had even processed his question. I wasn't at my best because I'd been working undercover all night.

"What do you guys do?" He blew a gum bubble. "Are you like private detectives and stuff?"

"We're mainly *the stuff*," I said. "Roy's our boss; he's the P.I."

"It must be a cool job."

"The coolest." Yawn.

Sheila signed for the parcel using his hand-held gizmo.

"I wouldn't mind being a P.I," he said. "It must be crazy exciting."

"There's plenty of the crazy, but not so much of the exciting."

"See ya, then." He scooted off.

"That poor young man." Sheila sighed.

"Delusional, you mean?"

"I meant his acne. Poor lad."

"What's in the parcel? More cigars?"

She nodded. "If Roy could see what smoking has done to Don, he wouldn't touch these things."

"Sorry, I should have asked you earlier. How is Don?"

"Oh, you know. Pretty much the same."

Sheila's husband had been seriously ill for months now, and although caring for him had taken its toll on her, she rarely complained.

"You shouldn't have to come in on a Saturday," I said.

"You've got enough to contend with at home."

"I don't mind. The extra money comes in handy. When Roy remembers to pay me, that is."

"What do you mean *when*? Doesn't he always pay you?"

"I had to remind him that I'd worked overtime last month. He probably just forgot."

"He was trying it on, more like."

"Why are you in today, Kat? You were working all last night."

"Roy said he wanted to see me this morning, but if he doesn't get here soon, he can whistle. I intend to be wrapped up in my bed by midday come what may."

Just then, the door burst open, and in walked Roy, dressed in his trademark Hawaiian shirt, shorts, flip flops and obligatory Rolex; the man had a fetish for them. He smelled of last night's booze, and as always, had a cigar in the corner of his mouth.

"Nice of you to bother," I said. "I've been up all night, but I still managed to get here on time."

"Shut it, Kat."

"Smoking isn't allowed in the building," I reminded him.

"Says who?"

"It's the law."

"Cigars don't count. And anyway, I don't pay you two to sit around gabbing."

"You don't pay me at all for Saturdays, and it sounds like you only pay Sheila when the mood takes you."

"Have you booked any more time on the Mason case this week?"

"It's *Marston*, and no, I haven't."

"Why not?"

"Because I was on another case last night, as you well know. And because it's a complete waste of time. Mr Marston isn't having an affair."

"I don't care if he's having an affair or not. I just need you to book as much time on the case as you can."

"Shouldn't we just tell the client the truth?"

"Don't be so naive. She doesn't want to hear the truth; she just wants proof her husband is cheating."

"Even if he isn't?"

"Precisely. And what's happening on the Premax case?"

"Like I said, I was there all night, but it was a waste of time. No one stole anything from those premises last night."

"Are you sure?"

"Positive. I would have seen it if they had."

"Unless you'd fallen asleep."

"If you want to do it yourself, Roy, be my guest."

"Watch your mouth, Kat. I can replace you any time I like."

"Don't have a go at me. I've had no sleep, and I'm in a foul mood."

"And I'm supposed to care why? I want you at Premax again on Monday night. And what about the Fulton case?"

"How am I supposed to work on that if I'm working the nightshift at Premax? I can't work twenty-four seven. You'll have to put someone else on it."

"What's wrong with working the Fulton case tomorrow?"

"It's Sunday."

"So what?"

"I can't work tomorrow. My kid sister is coming down

for the day."

"That's not my problem. I need you on the Fulton case."

"There's no way I'm working tomorrow."

"If you don't, don't bother coming in on Monday. Or ever again." He turned to Sheila. "Are those my cigars?" He snatched the parcel from her before she had a chance to answer.

"Are you staying to lend a hand, Roy?" I said.

"I can't. I have to go through the books because this place is haemorrhaging money, and I don't know why."

"Probably all your liquid lunches."

"Stop running your mouth off, Kat. Where are the books, Sheila?"

"In my drawer, but I haven't had time to bring them up to date."

"It doesn't matter."

"I could get them done by next weekend."

"Just give them to me, would you?"

She took several moth-eaten journals from her desk and handed them to him.

"I'll expect a report on the Fulton case by Monday, Kat." And with that, he stormed out.

"Screw you," I shouted at the closed door.

"Those books aren't up to date," Sheila said.

"Don't worry about it. He'll be too busy sacking me to worry about you or the books."

"What are you going to do about your sister?"

"What do you think? I haven't seen her since Christmas. I'm not going to cancel just because Roy's got his shorts in a twist."

***

Two hours later, the door flew open again.

"Is he in?" Westy worked for Roy on an as-needed basis. The man was six-six, and built like a tank.

I spoke up because I knew Sheila was intimidated by Westy. "He popped his head in earlier, but he's gone now."

"Did he leave my money?" He glared at Sheila, who handled all the accounts.

"Sorry, Mr West. He didn't leave it with me."

"That's twice this month he's stiffed me. I'm not standing for it, do you hear?"

"Leave off her, Westy." I stood up. "It's not her fault that Roy didn't leave your money."

"Yeah, well, I need it."

"You'd better take it up with Roy, then."

"Don't worry, I will. And if I don't get it, he'll be sorry." With that, he stormed out of the office, slamming the door behind him.

"I pity Roy if he doesn't have his money when Westy catches up with him," I said. "What has Westy been working on for Roy, anyway?"

Sheila shrugged. "He hasn't got around to telling me yet."

**

I loved it when Jen came down to see me, but I really wished she wouldn't insist on getting into St Pancras at stupid o'clock in the morning, especially on a Sunday. She'd caught the six o'clock train from Leeds because apparently it was much cheaper.

I spotted her at the top of the escalator; she'd had her hair cut into a short bob.

"Kat!" She waved.

"You look great." I pulled her in for a hug.

"*You* look like crap."

"Thanks, but what do you expect if you insist on arriving in the middle of the night? I like what you've done with your hair."

"Do you? Rick hates it."

"Of course he doesn't. That hubby of yours loves every square inch of you. And how's my favourite niece?"

"Take a look." She held out her phone and brought up the cutest photo you ever did see.

"She's grown."

"She's becoming a proper little madam. Mum says she reminds her of you at that age."

"How is Mum?"

"The same. She said to give you her love."

"Did you get anything to eat on the train?"

"Just a cup of tea."

"Good because I'm starving."

"Shall we go to Starbucks?" She pointed to the other side of the concourse.

"I'm not paying their prices, and besides, I need something more substantial. We could go to Joe's."

"Where's that?"

"It's a greasy spoon near to my office. It's only five minutes up the road."

"I haven't come all the way down here to go to a greasy spoon. I'm here for the glamour and bright lights."

Whenever Jen visited, which admittedly wasn't all that

often, we ended up going to places I wouldn't dream of going by myself. I generally tried to avoid the tourist hotspots like the plague. Normally, wild horses wouldn't have dragged me to Oxford Street, but that's the first place Jen made a beeline for.

"I wish we lived down here." She couldn't make her mind up which shop to drag me into next.

"You'd be begging to go back up north after a month."

"I envy you, Kat."

"Why would you envy me? You're the one with the doting husband and the beautiful daughter. To say nothing of the three-bed detached."

"Yeah, but your life is so much more exciting. I tell everyone that my sister is a private investigator."

"I'm not though. I'm just a dogsbody, and after tomorrow, I'll probably be a dogsbody looking for a new job."

"Why?"

"Roy wanted me to work today."

"You're not going to get the sack because of me, are you? You should have called and cancelled."

"No way I was going to do that."

"You can't afford to lose your job. What will you do?"

"I'll be fine. Chances are, he'll have forgotten by morning."

***

Jen had walked me ragged all day, and by three o'clock, I'd had enough. "Can we call it a day?"

"You never were much of a shopper, Kat."

"I've never had the money to be one. Do you want to

see Vi while you're down here?"

"Are you kidding? As far as Mum's concerned, Vi is the devil incarnate. If Mum found out that I'd visited her, she'd never talk to me again."

"Surely that's an incentive, isn't it?"

"Mum's not half as bad as you make her out to be."

"You didn't say that when you were living at home. You only married Rick to get away from her."

"I'm still not going to Vi's."

"She doesn't bite you know. How long is it since you saw her?"

"I don't remember. It must be five or six years."

"She's the only grandparent we have left. She won't be here forever."

"How old is she?"

"I'm not sure. She must be close to eighty by now."

"Do you still see her every day?"

"Not since I moved out of her place. It's usually once a week these days. She still talks about Dad a lot."

"I don't even remember him."

"That's hardly surprising. You were only five when he decided to sling his hook."

"Do you remember him?"

"I'm not sure. I feel like I know a lot about him, but most of that is probably just what Vi has told me."

"Why don't you call her Grandma?"

"Because she'd kill me if I did."

"I don't know how you do this journey twice a day, Kat."

We were on the DLR, headed for Lewford.

"This is the quiet period. You should see it at rush hour

during the week."

"Why don't you get somewhere closer to your office?"

"I can't afford anywhere closer. Truth be told, I can barely afford to live here."

"Is your new flat any better than the last place you had?"

"It's not as damp."

"That flat was horrible. I don't know how you lived there."

"Beggars can't be choosers. When I moved out of Vi's, it was the best I could afford. Come on, the next stop is us."

As we walked along the road towards my place, Jen's eyes were everywhere, as though she was expecting someone to jump out and steal her bag at any minute.

"You'll be okay." I tried to reassure her. "It's perfectly safe around here. In daylight, anyway."

"It's okay for you, Kat. You've got your kickboxing and the judo."

"I haven't done any judo since I moved down here, and I'm lucky if I get to go kickboxing more than a couple of times a month these days."

"I wish I'd done that fighting stuff now."

"I tried to get you to come with me when we were kids, but you were more interested in tap dancing."

"It was ballet, not tap."

"I remember all your trophies. You used to get one just for showing up."

"You were jealous because Mum used to come and watch my competitions."

"She didn't come and see any of mine."

"She was scared you were going to get hurt. You really

should give her a call, you know."

"I will."

"When?"

"Soon. Very soon."

"You said that the last time we spoke."

"And I meant it, but I've been crazy busy."

"One phone call wouldn't kill you, Kat. Or better still, you could come up and see her. You can stay at mine if you can't bear the thought of sleeping in your old room."

"I reckon Rick would have something to say about that."

"I don't know where you get the idea that he doesn't like you."

"He hates my guts. He's scared to death my evil ways are going to rub off on you."

"Now you're just being stupid."

"Spare some change, ladies?"

Jen looked sympathetically at the man sitting on the bottom step of the house, six doors down from my block of flats. Lying next to him, fast asleep, was a black Labrador. In between them, was a hat containing coins and at least one bank note.

"Get lost, Walt." I grabbed Jen's arm before she could take out her purse.

"You've got really hard since you moved down here," she said. "Why would you speak to a homeless guy like that?"

"Because he isn't homeless."

"That's typical of you, Kat. You think everyone is on the con, don't you?"

"Not everyone, but Walt definitely is. Do you see that house?"

"The one where he's sitting on the steps?"

"Yeah, that's where he lives."

"You mean he sleeps in the doorway at night?"

"No, I mean that's his house. He owns it."

"Don't be stupid."

"It's true. If the weather's fine, he comes out at seven o'clock, just in time to catch the morning rush hour, then he goes back inside for a coffee at ten. He's back on the steps at ten-thirty until lunchtime. Same in the afternoons."

"And you're sure about that?"

"Positive. When I first moved in, I threw him some change most mornings. That was until Robbie put me wise."

"Who's Robbie?"

"Do you see the greengrocer's shop across the road?"

"Yeah?"

"Robbie owns that. He's known Walt since they were kids."

"Wow! He's got some nerve, begging in front of his own house."

"He makes it pay too. Mind you, that's mainly down to The Brick."

"What brick?"

"That's the lab."

"The dog's called Brick?"

"He's not called *Brick*. He's called *The Brick*."

"Why is he called The Brick?"

"Beats me."

"Haven't you ever been tempted to ask?"

"I did once, but Walt said it would cost me twenty quid to find out, and I wasn't that interested."

"Is this it?" Jen stopped dead in her tracks only a few steps inside my flat.

"Gee, thanks."

"Sorry, I didn't mean, I—err, it's just that it's even smaller than your last place, isn't it?"

"It was a choice between small and dry, or large and damp. I couldn't afford large and dry."

"Is this the lounge as well as the kitchen, then?"

"Yeah. And that's my bedroom, and that's the bathroom."

"Just the one bedroom?"

"I can't afford two. Do you have any idea how much the rent is on this place?"

"A couple of hundred a month?"

"Dream on. You couldn't rent a wheelie bin for that around here. Multiply that by five, and you're getting close."

"That's ridiculous. We don't pay that much on our mortgage."

"Do you still want to move down here?"

"Where shall I put my stuff?"

"You can have the bedroom, and I'll sleep on the couch."

"I can't let you do that. I'll take the couch. Or we could share, like we used to when we were kids."

"No, thanks. I still remember how you snore."

***

The next morning, Jen offered to make her own way back to St Pancras, but I wasn't about to let her face the rush hour alone.

"Is it always as bad as that in the mornings?" By the time we reached the station, she looked shell-shocked.

"Not always. Sometimes it's much worse."

"I don't know how you do this every day."

"I thought you said you'd like to move down here?"

"I would, but I'd have to live somewhere more central."

"You'd need to win the lottery first."

"I'd better go. My train is boarding."

"Okay." We hugged. "Give my love to Rick and Alice."

"I will. And don't forget to give Mum a call."

"I won't."

"Promise?"

"Cross my heart."

"I hope you don't get the sack."

"I kind of hope I do."

That wasn't actually true. Although I could have gleefully strangled Roy most of the time, I needed the money. Hopefully, when I got to the office, he would have forgotten about his threat to give me my cards.

***

R.K. Investigations was located on the second floor of the Sidings Business Centre, which was on Heath Road — a side street equidistant between St Pancras and Euston stations. The building was old, cold and damp. Many moons ago, it had belonged to British Rail, but it was now home to dozens of small businesses.

When I arrived, there were two police cars in the small car park in front of the building. Seeing one there wouldn't have been particularly unusual because some of the businesses housed in the Sidings were more than a little shady. Two, though? What could have warranted that?

I didn't have long to wait to find out because it turned out that the police were in R.K. Investigations. One of them, Constable Joe Sharp, I recognised. He and I had had several run-ins over the last couple of years. He was standing next to Sheila's desk; she was in floods of tears.

"What's going on, Sharpy?"

"It's Constable Sharp to you."

"It's Roy!" Sheila sobbed.

"What's he done now?" I turned to Sharp. "What have you charged him with?"

"He hasn't been charged with anything. He's dead."

"What? How?"

"Mr King's body was discovered in the early hours of this morning. First indications are that he was murdered."

Chapter 2

A man, dressed in plain clothes, came out of Roy's office, and looked at me like I was something nasty he'd just trodden in.

"Who's this?"

"This is Kat Royle, Guv." Sharpy answered before I had the chance to speak. "She works for the deceased."

"What exactly happened to Roy?" I said.

"I ask the questions, Ms Royle."

"You can dispense with the *Ms Royle*. It's Kat. And who are you?"

"DCI Menzies. Would you come with me, please?" I followed him into the inner office where he sat at Roy's desk; he didn't invite me to take a seat. "Tell me, Kat, what exactly is it you did for Mr King?"

"Whatever he needed me to."

"Filing, making the tea, that sort of stuff?"

"No. Sheila does all the admin. I help on some of Roy's cases."

"You're a private investigator, then?" He smirked.

"Not really."

"But you just said you helped on the cases?"

"I do—err—did, but Roy would never have called me a P.I."

"What did he call you?"

"Every name under the sun."

"You and he didn't get along, then?"

"We weren't exactly bosom buddies. Are you going to tell me what happened to him? Who killed him?"

"We're still trying to establish that. Where were you last night between the hours of eleven and two?"

"In my flat."

"Which is where?"

"Lewford."

"Can anyone vouch for that?"

"Yeah. Jen."

"Your girlfriend?"

"My sister. She was visiting yesterday; she stayed the night."

"Where is she now?"

"I've just put her on a train back to Leeds."

"I assume you have her phone number in case we need to speak to her?"

"Do you think I killed Roy?"

"At this stage, we're simply trying to gather information. Your sister's phone number, please?"

I grabbed a pen from the desk and scribbled Jen's number onto a scrap of paper. "Is that all?"

"For now, yes, but I need you to give your details to Constable Sharp before you leave."

"*Leave*? Can't we stay here?"

"Not today. We'll be conducting a search of these offices."

"When can we come back?"

"It depends what we find, possibly tomorrow. Constable Sharp will keep you posted."

"When did the police show up?" I asked Sheila, over coffee in Joe's Café, which was just around the corner from the Sidings.

"Ten minutes after I arrived."

"Do you know how Roy was killed or where they found his body?"

She shrugged. "They wouldn't tell me anything."

"Do you reckon Westy might have done it? He was really angry when he came in here on Saturday."

"I don't know. It's possible, I suppose."

"Thank goodness this didn't happen while Jen was up here. It would have totally freaked her out."

"I'd forgotten your sister was coming down. How is she?"

"Fine. She said she'd like to move down here, but she soon changed her mind after she'd experienced rush hour, and discovered how much my rent is."

"What are we going to do now?" Sheila took a sip of coffee.

"We can't go back to the office until the police give us the all clear."

"I meant long term."

"I hadn't really thought about it."

"I suppose we should start looking for another job."

"That'll be fun."

"You'll be okay, Kat. You've got bags of experience."

"Doing what? Being Roy's gopher?"

"You're a lot more than that. You've run lots of cases single-handed."

"Who's going to believe that? It's not like I can ask Roy for a reference, is it?"

"Do you think anyone will have told his daughter?"

"Anne? The police will have informed her, won't they?"

"I hope so." Sheila checked her watch. "I'd better get going. Don has a hospital appointment in an hour. What are you going to do now?"

"There's not much I can do. I might just head back to the flat and check out the job websites."

The journey back was much better because the rush hour was long since over, so I was able to get a seat all the way home.

As I made my way from the tube station, there was no sign of Walt or The Brick; I assumed he must be on his mid-morning tea break.

I lived on the third floor of seven, and I'd just stepped out of the lift when my next-door neighbour, the Widow Manning, came hurrying over.

"Kat, have you heard? He's dead."

"I didn't know you knew Roy?"

"Who's Roy?"

"Isn't that who you're talking about?"

"No. I meant Walt."

"How?"

"Heart attack, I think. Someone found him slumped on the begging step just over an hour ago."

"Poor old Walt. What's happened to The Brick?"

"What brick?"

"That's his dog's name."

"I never knew that. I've got him in my flat. He was wandering around in the road, so I brought him up here before he got himself run over."

"What are you going to do with him?"

"I don't know. If I take him to the pound, they'll put him down. He's too old and ugly to rehome."

"Couldn't you keep him?"

"I'd like to. I miss having a dog since my Buster died. The problem is I won't be able to take him for a walk. My old legs aren't up to it. What about you?"

"Me?"

"If I take him in, would you walk him occasionally?"

"I'm out at work in the week."

"You could do it before you go, and then again when you get back. He's an old dog, so he won't need to go very far."

"I'm not sure about this."

"Please, Kat." She looked me up and down. "You could do with the exercise."

"Thanks."

"So, will you do it?"

"Do I have a choice?"

"No, not really."

***

I phoned Jen. "I'm just checking that you got back okay."

"Yeah. The reservations were messed up, but I managed to get a seat anyway. I was going to wait until tonight to call you because I thought you'd be busy."

"It's been a funny kind of a day so far."

"How so?"

I told her about Roy's murder and Walt's heart attack.

"Oh gosh. Do they know who murdered your boss?"

"If they do, they aren't saying anything. They even asked if I had an alibi."

"Seriously?"

"It was just routine. Nothing to worry about."

"Where does that leave you now?"

"How do you mean?"

"You'll be out of a job, won't you?"

"Looks like it."

"You should come home."

"This *is* my home, Jen. I'll find another job."

"Doing what?"

"I don't know. I'll work something out. Do me a favour, would you?"

"What?"

"Don't tell Mum about any of this. I don't need her on my back too."

"Okay, but promise you'll think about coming back if you can't find anything."

"I can't come home because I have a dog now."

"How come?"

"The Widow Manning has taken Walt's Labrador in, but she wants me to take him for a walk occasionally."

"Who's the Widow Manning?"

"The old lady who lives just down the corridor."

"Why do you call her that?"

"It's what everyone calls her."

"I suppose the exercise would do you good. Anyway, I'd better go. I have to pick up Alice from Mum's."

"Give her a kiss from me."

"I will. Be careful."

"I always am."

***

I couldn't be bothered to make dinner, and besides, the only thing I had in was a couple of Pot Noodles.

The Gerbil and Oyster, my local pub, was a stone's throw from my building.

"Hi, Kat. How goes it?" Kenny, the landlord, had Billy on his shoulder.

No, they weren't acrobats; Billy was a parrot or parakeet—I never did know (or care) what the difference was.

"Sod off!" the parrot said.

"Nice to see you, too, Billy."

"Sod off!"

"You really do need to teach him to say something different, Kenny."

"He does, but he's under strict instructions not to repeat it in public. Your usual?"

"Yeah, and can I see the menu?"

"You're hilarious, as always."

The sign outside the pub said they served food, but what it didn't say was that the menu comprised of only three choices: fish and chips, scampi and chips, and ham sandwiches with or without chips.

"Don't you think it might be an idea to expand your offerings?" I said, more out of hope than expectation.

"Why would we bother? There's everything on there that a person could want."

"There's nothing for vegetarians for a start."

"Of course there is: Chips."

"Just chips?"

"Plus a slice of bread if they want one. You haven't gone and turned veggie, have you, Kat?"

"Me? No. I'll have the fish and chips."

"Peas?"

"Do you have garden peas?"

"No, just mushy."

"In that case, I won't bother."

Don't get me wrong. Normally, I was a big fan of the mushy pea, but not those served up in the Gerbil and Oyster. I mean, since when were peas brown?

I found a seat near the bar; it wasn't difficult because the place was deserted. Most of Kenny's customers arrived after seven, and were still in there long after the doors were locked at eleven. That's when the card games started. At least, that's what I'd been told by Robbie, the greengrocer.

I had no expectation of seeing my meal any time soon because Becky, Kenny's partner, made all the meals from frozen. She'd recently invited me to see her new chest freezer, and I'd done my best to look suitably impressed.

"Isn't that your boss?" Kenny shouted from behind the bar. "On the news."

I had to shuffle my chair a few inches to the left so that I could see the wall-mounted TV. Sure enough, they were running a news item about Roy's murder.

"Yeah, that's him."

"Who murdered him?"

"No idea."

"Where does that leave you?"

"I'm not sure. Looking for a job, I guess."

I was half way through my fish and chips when I sensed someone hovering close to my table.

"Leo? What do you want?"

"That's no way to greet an old friend, is it?"

Leo and I had been an item, briefly. He'd seemed nice enough at first. That was until I discovered his wife thought so too. Somehow, he'd conveniently forgotten to mention her.

"Do you mind? I'm trying to eat my dinner."

"It looks nice. Can I nick a chip?" He reached for one, but I slapped his hand away.

"I asked what you wanted, Leo?"

"I heard about Roy, so I thought I'd check that you were okay."

"You've checked. I'm okay. Bye."

"You're a hard woman, Kat. We had some good times together, didn't we? Don't you remember that Sunday when we spent the whole—"

"I don't remember anything about our time together. I barely remember you. Now, if you don't mind, I'd like to eat my dinner in peace."

"Do they know who murdered Roy?"

"Not as far as I'm aware."

"You could always move in with me until they catch them. It would be safer."

"I think Gina might have something to say about that."

"We're on a trial separation."

"She kicked you out more like." I grinned. "Where are you staying?"

"At my brother's gaff."

"Bobby? I thought he was living in a squat?"

"He is, but it's alright. They've got electricity and everything."

"Tempting as that is, I think I'll stay put."

"Your loss." He shrugged. "You've got my number if you change your mind."

I was just on my way out of the pub when I spotted Rose Hawkins, sitting in a corner, all by herself. Rose was one of Lewford's most colourful characters. She ran the fruit and veg stall on Lewford market, and spent most of her time shouting out the price of bananas. Or potatoes — or whatever else she happened to be trying to shift on that particular day. Because she spent so much of her time shouting, she sometimes forgot where she was, and would still yell during a normal conversation. Rose was Lewford born and bred; there was no one she didn't know, and everyone knew her. I couldn't remember the last time I'd seen her sitting all by herself, and I'd certainly never known her to be so quiet.

"Hey, Rose."

"Hi, Kat."

"Are you okay? What are you doing, sitting in the corner all on your lonesome?"

"I'm alright."

She clearly wasn't. "What's up? Has something happened? It's not your Fred, is it?"

"Nah, he's alright. He's down the snooker hall with his brother."

"Something's wrong."

"It's me old mum."

"Oh, I'm sorry. She's not — ?"

"Nah, nothing like that." Rose pointed to the chair next to her. "Grab a pew."

"Can I get you another drink first?"

"I'm alright, thanks." She waited until I was seated. "I got a phone call last night, to say Mum was in hospital. She's eighty-five, so I feared the worst. They wouldn't tell me much over the phone, so I got a cab and shot straight over there. She was in a right state. If I get my hands on the scumbag, I'll rip his nuts off and choke him with them."

"Who? What happened?"

"Some guy showed up at her door and said he was there about the leccy. I'd told her to always ask for ID, and she said she had, and that he'd shown her his card. It could have been anything cos her eyesight ain't up to much. Anyways, she lets him in, and he checks the meter, supposedly. Then, after he'd left, she saw that one of the drawers in her sideboard wasn't shut properly. He'd taken all of her jewellery. She's shook up something rotten."

"Was it worth very much?"

"Not really. Five hundred quid tops. It's not the money. My dad gave her most of that stuff. It meant the world to her."

"Is she still in hospital?"

"Yeah. They said they wanted to keep an eye on her for a couple of days. The thing is, I'm not sure if she's going to be okay in that house by herself now. Her and my dad lived there almost forty years, but this has really shaken her."

"What do the police have to say about it?"

"Not much, as you'd expect. Don't get me wrong, they were very good with Mum, and they're obviously as disgusted with whoever did this as I am. But, realistically, they don't have the resources to devote to something like this."

I stayed with Rose for another half hour until she'd got it all out of her system.

"I hope your mum's okay. Give her my best wishes."

"Thanks, Kat. See you around."

***

Back at the flat, the Widow Manning was waiting for me in the ground floor hallway. The black lab was lying at her feet.

"Thank goodness you're back, Kat. He needs to go for a walk."

"It looks like he's asleep to me."

"He must need to go. He hasn't done anything all day."

"Are we talking number one or number two here?"

"Both, I imagine. Here." She handed me a small plastic bag.

"What's this for?"

"What do you think?"

"Gross. What do I do with the bag afterwards?"

"There's a bin at the far end of the road, near the park." She handed me his lead. "You can't miss it. It's a big red thing."

"Okay." I gave a gentle tug on the lead, and the dog followed me out of the door.

I was just wondering where I should take him, when he began to pull on the lead. He seemed to know where he wanted to go, so I gave him his head, and he led the way to the park.

Once there, I let him off the lead, and he shuffled over to a clump of bushes. He was an old dog, and moved at a slow pace, so I was easily able to keep up with him. Ten minutes and lots of sniffing later, he got down to the main business of the day.

Seriously? For a moment there I began to wonder if the bag was going to be big enough.

While I put the bag into the red bin, which smelt like Hades had just farted, the dog refocussed his energy on sniffing.

"Come on, boy!" I started towards him, but he saw the lead, and walked in the opposite direction. "Come here!" He ignored me again, so I tried to grab him, but even though he was slow, he was crafty, and he managed to duck out of reach every time.

Ten minutes later, and I was still chasing shadows. In desperation, I shouted, "The Brick! Come here!"

Much to my amazement, he came trotting over to me, and stood stock-still while I clipped on his lead.

"That's a great name." A man with a golden retriever grinned at me.

Chapter 3

The next morning, I was starving, but all I had in were a couple of slices of bread and an egg. I considered nipping out to Geordie's for one of their famous full English breakfasts, but as I didn't have a clue when and where my next pay cheque was coming from, I had to watch the pennies. So, egg on toast it was.

Breakfast finished, I added the plate to the ever-growing pile of pots waiting to be washed. The dishwasher had broken a week earlier, and I hadn't yet come to terms with having to revert to washing them by hand. Maybe, if I said a prayer to the electrical appliance fairies, they would mend it for me.

My phone rang; caller ID showed an unknown number. It was probably some idiot trying to sell me something.

"Yes?"

"It's Constable Sharp."

"Morning, Sharpy."

"I just wanted to let you know that we've released your offices."

"Great. Did you find anything?"

"I'm not at liberty to discuss an on-going investigation."

"Go on, Sharpy. You can tell me. I won't tell anyone."

"Goodbye, Kat."

"Spoilsport."

I called Sheila.

"It's Kat."

"Hi. Are you okay?"

"Fine. The police just called. We can go back to the office."

"That was quick. Did they say if they'd found anything?"

"They wouldn't tell me."

"Is there any point in us going back there, Kat? Now that Roy is dead, I mean?"

"I'm not sure, but I don't know what else to do."

"The thing is, I'm going to be at the hospital with Don all day today, but I should be okay to come in tomorrow."

"Okay, I'll see you then."

As soon as I stepped out of the door, the Widow Manning appeared in her doorway; she'd obviously been listening out for me.

"The dog needs a walk."

"Another one? I only took him last night."

"Could *you* manage on only one pee a day?"

"Point taken, but I really do have to get to the office."

"Best hurry, then." She handed me his lead, and The Brick took that as his cue to drag me to the park.

"Is that really his name?" It was the same man I'd seen the previous day; the one with the golden retriever and the smug look.

"Sorry?"

"Is your dog really called Brick?"

"It's The Brick, actually."

"Were you drunk when you named him?"

"He isn't my dog. Not all of him, anyway."

"Which part belongs to you?"

"I share him with the Widow Manning."

"Does everyone in your life have a weird name?"

"What's *your* dog's name?"

"Miles."

"What kind of name is that to give to a self-respecting dog?"

"If he could talk, I'm pretty sure he'd say he preferred Miles to The Brick. I'm Graham, by the way."

"Kat."

"How come I haven't seen you in here before yesterday?"

"I didn't have a dog until then."

"How come you have one, or part of one, now?"

"He used to belong to a guy named Walt, who lived a few doors down from me, but he dropped dead of a heart attack."

"Do you mean the homeless guy? I knew I'd seen that dog somewhere before."

"Walt wasn't actually homeless."

"How can you possibly know that?"

"You know the house where he used to beg?"

"Yeah?"

"Walt owned it."

"Are you sure?"

"Positive."

"What a nerve. So, you've taken his dog in? Quite the good Samaritan, aren't you?"

"Not really. It was my neighbour who took him in."

"The Widow Manning?"

"That's right. She isn't very good on her feet, so she's recruited me for walkies duty."

"Welcome to our little community. There are several regulars who come in here." He checked the time on his phone. "I'd better be going. Time and tide and all that."

While I'd been talking, The Brick had deposited an

obscene amount of number two right next to a patch of nettles.

"You did that deliberately, didn't you?"

He gave me a butter wouldn't melt look, but I knew better.

***

I went to the office as though it was just another normal day, but as soon as I walked through the door, reality smacked me in the face. What did I think I was doing there? I should be pounding the streets, looking for another job.

My mind was still in something of a fuzz when I walked through to Roy's office. I rarely went in there, and when I did, it was usually because he wanted to give me a dressing-down about something or other.

It occurred to me that he might have left some personal items in his desk drawers. I could at least make myself useful by gathering them together for whoever eventually came around to collect them.

I'd no sooner taken a seat at his desk when someone came into the outer office.

"Hello? Kat? Sheila? Anyone home?"

It was Roy's daughter, Anne.

"Through here!"

"Hi, Kat." Her eyes were red and puffy.

"Sorry." I jumped up, embarrassed that she'd found me sitting in her father's seat. "I was just checking for any of your dad's personal items."

"Don't be silly. Sit down." She took a seat at the other

side of the desk. "It's not like he's going to be needing the desk, is it?"

"How are you doing?"

"Not great. I was the one who found him."

"I had no idea. I'm so sorry."

"He called me every night, you know. Without fail. When he didn't call on Sunday, I knew something was wrong, so I went straight around there." It took her a couple of minutes to compose herself enough to carry on. "He was lying on the kitchen floor. There was blood. So much—" Her words drifted away.

"That must have been terrible for you."

"I know he was a pain, Kat, and he wasn't a brilliant father, but he was all I had."

"The police will soon catch whoever did it."

"Will they, though? I wish I shared your confidence. They reckon it was a burglary gone wrong, but that's crap."

"Have they said why they think it was a burglary?"

"Because, according to them, the living room had been trashed. But it hadn't. One chair and the coffee table had been tipped over—that was all."

"Was anything taken?"

"Just the watch he was wearing."

"The Rolex?"

"Yeah, but if it was a burglary, why didn't they take the others? Dad had seven altogether; one for each day of the week. It's not like they were difficult to find; they were all in his bedside cabinet. I could never understand why he spent so much money on those stupid things when he was living in that hovel."

"Are you here to pick up his stuff?"

"No. There's nothing here that I want. I came to see you."

"Oh?"

"I want you to find out what really happened to Dad, Kat."

"Me? I've never worked on a murder investigation."

"I'll pay you."

"It isn't that. I wouldn't take your money, anyway."

"Please. I don't trust the police. It's obvious that they're only going to put the bare minimum of resources into this. Dad always said you were the best investigator he'd ever worked with."

"No, he didn't." I laughed. "He was always telling me how useless I was."

"That was just his way of making sure you didn't ask for a raise. You should have done. He'd have given it to you."

"Are you being serious? Did he really say that?"

"Honestly. He really rated you."

"Wow. I don't know what to say."

"Say you'll find Dad's murderer."

"I'm willing to give it a go, but I wouldn't want to build your hopes up."

"Just say you'll try."

"Of course I will. Would it be okay if I continued to work out of this office while I do?"

"Why don't you just stay here permanently?"

"What do you mean?"

"You should keep the agency going."

"Me?"

"Have you got any other plans?"

"Not really. I was going to start looking for another

job."

"What do you have to lose by trying to make a go of this place? You can still look for a job if it doesn't work out."

"By rights, the business belongs to you now that Roy has gone."

"I have absolutely no interest in it. It's not worth anything, is it?"

"I wouldn't have thought so. Roy could barely make payroll each month."

"That's what I thought. If you want to give it a go, I'm fine with that. The name would still work."

"Sorry?"

"R.K. Investigations. Royle, Kat—it's close enough."

"I hadn't even thought of that."

"So you'll do it?"

"Yes, but I won't take any money for working on your dad's case."

"Okay. If you need me to sign any paperwork, just let me know."

"Will do. Thanks, Anne."

No sooner had Anne left than I got a visit from Tommy Hill, landlord of the Sidings. He was an okay kind of guy, but he never missed a trick when it came to maximising his profits.

"Hey, Kat. I see you've already claimed Roy's office. I thought I should drop by to find out when you'll be vacating this place."

"It's only been a day, Tommy."

"So says the woman sitting at her boss's desk. I just need a rough idea, so I know when I can re-let it."

"I might try to keep the agency running."

"Can you do that?"

"His daughter is cool with it. In fact, it was her idea. And, I've already worked on a lot of Roy's cases. Would that be okay with you?"

"I guess so. It would save me the trouble of having to find a new tenant, but you'll have to make sure you come up with the rent on time."

"When's it due next?"

"A week on Tuesday."

"Don't I get some kind of free introductory period?"

"No chance. Do you want to stay on or not?"

"You're a hard man, but yes."

"Okay, I'll get the paperwork changed, and bring it up for you to sign. What's the new business going to be called?"

"I thought I'd keep the same name. Continuity and all that."

"Fair enough." He offered his hand. "Best of luck, Kat."

"Thanks, Tommy."

Not long after the landlord had left, the phone on Roy's desk rang. As I went to answer it, I wondered how long it would be before I stopped thinking of it as *Roy's* desk and considered it to be mine.

"R.K. Investigations. Kat Royle speaking."

"This is Ted Fulton. Roy King said that someone from your office would be contacting me, but I heard on the TV that he'd been murdered. I thought I'd better check what was going on, and if I should make alternative arrangements?"

"That won't be necessary, Mr Fulton. Roy had already asked me to take on your case. I would have been in touch yesterday, but as you can imagine, things were a little difficult."

"But the business is still operational?"

"Absolutely. Would you prefer to pop into the office, or for me to come out and see you?"

"If you could come to me, that would be great."

"Okay. I can make it anytime today, to suit you."

"I have a meeting in a few minutes. How about first thing this afternoon? Say one o'clock?"

"That's fine. I have your address on file, so I'll see you then."

"Okay."

My first client!

I didn't have time to celebrate because my mobile rang.

"Kat? It's Sonya. I thought I should check how you are. I heard about Roy."

"I'm okay. The police have just let me back in the office."

"Are you there now?"

"Yeah."

"Is it okay if I pop down for a coffee? You can tell me all about it."

"Sure. Why not? I don't have to worry about Roy giving me a hard time now. Does saying that make me a horrible person?"

"Yeah, but I won't tell anyone if you don't. I'll be down in two ticks."

Sonya worked part-time at Buyvrator, one of the many small businesses located in the Sidings. As its name suggested, the business sold adult toys.

The kettle had just boiled when she walked into the outer office. "Kat?"

"I'm through here."

"Are we having our drinks in here?" She glanced around Roy's office.

"What's wrong? Are you afraid his ghost might be watching?"

"It just feels a bit weird."

"Black, one sugar?" I held up the coffee jar.

"Yes, please."

"What are your plans now?" She asked once we were seated at the desk.

"I'm going to try to keep the business going and see what happens."

"Thank goodness for that. Who would I chat to if you left?"

"You'd still have Craig." I grinned.

"Don't talk to me about that loser."

Sonya and Craig had had an on/off relationship for over a year. These days it seemed to be more off than on.

"What's he done this time?"

"The pig stood me up for West Ham. It wasn't even a first team match."

"Are you still enjoying the job?"

"Yeah, I love it. I get a great discount too. I just wish they could give me more hours. I'm looking for a second job. If you hear of anything, let me know, will you?"

"Sure."

"I always thought you and I had a lot in common, Kat."

"In what way?"

"We both work with dicks. I sell them, and you used to take orders from one."

"That's a bit harsh."

"But true?"

"Absolutely."

"What about Sheila? Will she be staying on?"

"I hope so. She doesn't know yet that Anne has said I can continue to run the agency. I'll give her a call tonight."

"All systems go, then. Are you going to change the name?"

"I don't see the point. It's just additional expense, and R.K. works just fine anyway."

"It's almost like it was destined to be."

"I probably ought to invest in a few business cards, though. I've never needed them before because Roy has always been the one who brought in the work."

"You should go and see Vic. He'll see you right."

"Who's that?"

"He's on the third floor. The office next to the gents' toilets."

"What's the name on the door?"

"He doesn't seem to have a business name, but he does all kinds of printing. Very reasonable prices. Tell him I sent you."

Just then, my phone rang, so Sonya mouthed a goodbye, and slipped out of the office.

"Kat? It's Mrs Marston."

"Hi."

"I was hoping I might have heard from you by now. When I spoke to Roy last week, he said he thought you were close to getting something on Roger."

The moment of truth had arrived. Did I continue to string the poor woman along, just to bump up the bill, or did I tell her the truth?

"I'm not sure if you heard, but Roy King was murdered on Sunday night."

"What? Oh, my goodness. I had no idea. I'm so sorry."

"The truth is, Mrs Marston, I've followed your husband on and off for the last two weeks, and I'm almost certain that he isn't seeing anyone else."

"But what about those times when you weren't following him? He might have been up to something then?"

"That's always possible, but I've had a lot of experience of working on adultery cases, and I can tell you that it's usually very obvious when someone is cheating. I genuinely don't think your husband is. Can I ask why you're suspicious of him?"

"Nothing in particular. It's just a feeling I can't shake."

"It's entirely up to you of course. I can continue to follow him, and report back if that's what you want, or —"

"You really don't think he's seeing anyone else?"

"I'm almost certain he isn't. I would have spotted something by now if he was."

"Maybe you're right. Perhaps it's just my overactive imagination. I suppose I could see how it goes between us, and if anything happens to raise more doubts, I could contact you again. Or will you be shutting the business down, after what's happened?"

"No, I intend to continue running it."

"That's what I'll do, then. And, of course, I'll need to pay your bill for the work you've done to date. Are you still based in the same offices?"

"Yes."

"Okay, I'll drop the payment off in the next day or so."

Well, that was clever. My first executive decision as the new owner of the agency had been to convince a client that she didn't need my services. I wasn't sure Roy would have approved of my new business strategy.

Chapter 4

I decided to take Sonya's advice, and went in search of Vic the printer. Clients would expect me to have some kind of business card, so the sooner I ordered them, the better.

Just as Sonya had said, there was no name on the door adjacent to the gents' toilets. I knocked, but there was no reply, so I tried the door and it opened.

"Hello? Anyone in?"

The office, if you could call it that, was a room without a stick of furniture in it. I was just beginning to think that Vic must have moved out, when a door at the back opened and a man appeared.

It was only then that I realised I'd seen Vic before, but I'd always thought of him as Half-An-Ear. I'd walked past him a few times in the corridors, and I'd often wondered how he'd lost the top half of his right ear.

"Can I help you?" He had what sounded like a Brummie accent.

"Are you Vic?"

"Depends who's asking."

"I'm Kat Royle. Sonya said I should come and see you about some printing."

"Naughty Sonya?" He grinned. "Are you two in the same line of business?"

"No, I'm a—err—" I hesitated. "I'm a P.I, I guess."

"Aren't you sure?"

"Yeah, I'm definitely a P.I."

"What are you after, Kat?"

"I just need some business cards."

"How many do you want?"

"I don't know. How many do people normally order?"

"It varies, but five hundred should keep you going for a while. Do you have a logo?"

"No, nothing like that."

"I'll knock one up for you. No extra charge for a new customer. What else do you want on the cards?"

"Just the name of the business: R.K. Investigations, the address and my phone number."

"Don't you think you should have *your* name on there too?"

"Oh yeah. I'd forgotten about that."

"What about social media? Website, Facebook, Twitter, that kind of thing?"

"I don't have any of those."

"You'll need to get that sorted pretty sharpish. A business isn't a business these days without all of that stuff."

This from the man who didn't even have his business's name on the door.

"I'll get on it. Soon. Any idea when I can expect the cards?"

"You can have them tomorrow if you like. Twenty-five quid okay?"

"I guess so."

"Tomorrow it is, then."

The only thing I'd had to eat that day was the egg on toast I'd had for breakfast, and my stomach was making its displeasure known. Ideally, I would have liked to nip across the road to the Dog and Duck to treat myself to their midweek carvery, but my finances wouldn't run to that. Instead, I had to make do with the school canteen.

The café, which was located on the top floor of the business centre, was actually called Mary's Diner, but everyone knew it as the school canteen. Before starting her own business, Mary had worked at a number of different schools over a period spanning twenty years. When she'd moved into the commercial sector, she'd seen no reason to change the tried and tested methods that she'd used to feed generations of schoolkids. That probably explained why the café was rarely more than one quarter full.

Mary didn't believe in either menus or choice. You had what you were given, and if you didn't eat it all, you could expect to receive some caustic comment on your way out.

"What's that, Mary?" I pointed.

"Yorkshire pudding. What does it look like?"

I resisted the temptation to give her an honest answer, but only because she was wielding an enormous carving knife.

"You've forgotten your broccoli," she shouted after me, as I headed to the till.

"I don't like it."

"Broccoli!" She pointed again—this time with the knife.

I didn't argue. Instead, I put the smallest piece I could find onto my plate.

Eating lunch in Mary's Diner brought it all streaming back to me: Mr West, the physics teacher, who spent all lunchtime picking his nose. Wendy Rowling, and her insistence on having a separate plate for each vegetable. Joan Carver, the prefect who used to get some kind of kick out of making my life a misery. And who could forget Nigel Lane who got his rocks off by deliberately spilling custard down the blouse of any girl who made the mistake of getting too close to his table.

Whoever said school days were the happiest of your life obviously hadn't attended Haywood High.

I was trying to figure out where best to secrete the broccoli when I noticed a young man, going from table to table. Whatever he was selling, no one was buying. He was tall, very slim, and probably about twenty years old. And as for his hair, I'd never seen anything quite like it. How did he get it to stick out at that angle?

"Excuse me." He'd reached my table.

Before he could start his pitch, I got in first. "Do you like broccoli?"

"Sorry?"

"Broccoli? Do you like it?"

"No, it brings me out in hives."

"You're not much use then, are you?"

"I'm looking for a job."

"What kind of job?"

"Anything. I don't mind. I'm good with computers, numbers and stuff. I used to be a bit of a hacker, but I'm reformed now."

"That's reassuring."

"Have you got anything for me?"

"Sorry, no."

"Can I leave you my CV, just in case?"

"If you like, but it's unlikely I'll have anything in the foreseeable future."

"Thanks." He handed me an A4 sheet of paper from his folder. "I'm Zero."

"You're never going to get a job if you don't use your real name."

"That is my real name."

"Honestly?"

"Yeah. Zero Smith. My mum says she wanted to give me an interesting first name to compensate for my boring surname."

"Right. Well, good luck with the job hunting."

"Thanks."

Zero handed out a few more CVs, and then made his way out of the canteen. All I had to do now was to get out of there before Mary spotted that I'd left the broccoli. I bided my time, and after a couple of minutes, Ron and Don, who ran the dog-sitting business on the ground floor, went to the counter. While Mary was busy serving them, I made a dash for the door.

***

If Roy had still been alive, I would have taken a cab to Fulton's offices. He would have moaned about my expenses claim, but then he moaned about everything I did. Now that all the expenses were going to come out of my pocket, there was no way I'd be taking cabs. Not for the foreseeable future at least.

Two tube journeys, and a ten-minute walk later, I was at the offices of Fulton Associates.

"Can I help you?" Judging by the expression on her face, the woman on reception obviously thought I should have taken the tradesmen's entrance.

"Ted Fulton is expecting me. I'm Kat Royle."

She checked her computer. "You'd better take a seat. I'll let Mr Fulton know you're here."

The selection of magazines was straight out of a

dentist's waiting room, so I gave them a miss.

"Kat?" The man was tall, dark and very ordinary. His suit was expensive, but probably not as expensive as his teeth.

"Mr Fulton?"

"It's Ted. Would you come with me?" He led the way to a bank of lifts. "Did Roy King brief you?" He hit the button for the sixth floor.

"Not fully. Something about your partner, I believe?"

"That's right. He's disappeared." The lift doors opened in front of a huge glass-fronted office. "Can I get you anything to drink?"

The small bar in one corner of the office was better stocked than the Gerbil and Oyster.

"I'll take a cola if you have one."

He handed me a bottle and a glass, and then poured himself a very large whisky.

"Take a seat." He gestured to one of the white sofas. "How long have you worked for R.K. Investigations?"

"Just over six years."

He sank half of the whisky. "And you plan on keeping the business going?"

"That's right."

"My partner's name is Mike Dale. We've worked together for almost ten years."

"What exactly is your business?"

"We're financial consultants. Mike and I are partners."

"How come his name isn't above the door?"

"I started by myself originally. Mike bought into the business about a year later, but he insisted that I didn't change the company name. He prefers to keep a low profile."

"When did he go missing?"

"The weekend before last. He left work as usual on Friday evening, and no one has seen him since. I've tried to phone him a hundred times, but the calls all go to voicemail."

"Does he live with anyone?"

"No. He got divorced a couple of years back. His ex-wife moved to the States with her new partner about six months ago."

"Children? Other family?"

"They didn't have any kids, and there's no one else as far as I know. Mike's an only child; both his parents died several years ago."

"Did the divorce affect him badly?"

"No. If anything, I'd say it came as a relief. Those two should never have got together in the first place."

"Has he been seeing anyone since the divorce?"

"Nothing that has lasted more than a few months. I seem to remember the last woman he was seeing was called Liz, or Lisa."

"What about work? Has he been under more pressure than usual recently?"

"No. Certainly nothing he couldn't handle. Mike's a happy-go-lucky sort of a guy. Not much worries him."

"Enemies? Personal or business?"

"None. He's not the kind of man to make enemies."

"Have you reported him missing to the police?"

"No. I wasn't sure they'd be interested, and to be honest, we could do without the bad publicity. That's why I contacted your office. A business associate used your agency last year; he was the one who recommended you."

We talked for another twenty minutes about Mike Dale

and the business, but I didn't learn anything of any significance.

"Okay. I'll probably have more questions over the coming days."

"Call me anytime."

"Before I go, would it be possible to take a look at Mike's office?"

"Of course. I'll get his PA, Tasmin, to show you around if that's alright?"

"That'll be fine."

Tasmin glided in on the tallest heels I'd ever seen, and yet she made it look like she was walking in flats.

"Hi. I'm Tas."

"Kat."

"Mike's office is on the other side of this floor. Can I get you a drink on the way over?"

"Not for me, thanks. What kind of man is Mike?" I asked as we made our way across the floor.

"He seems okay."

"*Seems*?"

"Didn't Ted tell you? I've only been here for a month."

"No, he didn't mention that."

"To tell you the truth, I haven't seen very much of Mike. He spends most of his time out of the office."

"Did you see him on the Friday before last? The day he went missing?"

"Yes, he was in all day that day, which is quite unusual." She came to a halt outside another glass-fronted office, similar to the one I'd just been in with Ted Fulton. "This is Mike's office. Shall I wait out here?"

"No, come in, please."

The first thing that struck me was how empty the room felt compared to Ted's. The only furniture in the huge office was a desk, a chair and a leather sofa next to the window.

"Has this office always been so sparsely furnished?"

"Since I've been here, yes. When I first started, I assumed they must have taken out some of the furniture while the office was being decorated, but it turned out that this is how Mike prefers it."

"Doesn't he have a computer?"

"Yeah, a laptop. It's usually on his desk."

"Does he sometimes take it home with him?"

"I'd never known him to. When I mentioned to Ted that it was missing, he said it had been taken by I.T. for repair."

Before I left, I had Tas give me Mike Dale's address and phone number.

"Thanks for your help, Tas."

"No problem. Do you think he's okay?"

"That's what I intend to find out."

"I hope so. This is the best job I've ever had; I'd hate to lose it already." She blushed. "Sorry, that's a terrible thing to say, isn't it? Obviously, I hope Mike's okay too."

"I understand. Just one last thing, could you take me to your I.T. department?"

"Sure. It's on the floor below this one."

Tas introduced me to Greg Crawley, the head of I.T. He was the typical I.T. geek: sandals and a goatee.

"This will only take a minute, Greg," I said. "Can you tell me what was wrong with Mike Dale's computer?"

"Sorry?"

"I believe you had it collected from his office for repair?"

"I don't think so. Let me just double-check." He tapped a few keys on his computer. "No, there's no record of a fault call for Mike Dale."

"Okay. Thanks very much."

There was something about this case that didn't pass my sniff test. Fulton had said he was concerned about bad publicity, but it struck me as weird that he wouldn't have reported his partner's disappearance to the police. And why had he told Tas that Mike Dale's laptop had been taken for repair by the I.T. department when that obviously wasn't true?

Chapter 5

I was just about to get onto the tube when I received a text message from Christine Mather. She had been one of the first friends I'd made when I moved down to London. For a while back then, we'd been inseparable. Then she'd met Ralph.

The last time I'd seen her, she'd told me she'd never speak to me again, and that I was dead to her. Yes, she actually did say those very words. That was two years ago, when I'd made the mistake of thinking she'd want to know that her good-for-nothing boyfriend was cheating on her with a woman named Fiona. Unfortunately, I hadn't allowed for the fact that she was so smitten with Ralph that she wouldn't hear a bad word said against him. Not even from the person who she'd insisted was her BFF. Yes, she'd really said that too.

When I'd told Christine about Ralph and Fiona, she'd accused me of being jealous and of fancying Ralph myself. Seriously? I'd rather have dated the guy who sells wet fish on the local market. It's not that I have anything against wet fish per se, but the guy who sells it is so ugly it should be illegal. At first, I'd thought she was joking, but she was deadly serious. She'd stormed out of the pub, but not before telling me that hell would freeze over before she spoke to me again.

Apparently, the underworld was currently experiencing something of a cold snap.

Christine's text said simply:

Can we meet, please? V important.

If I was the vindictive sort, I would have ignored the message, or sent her a snippy reply, but that's not who I am. And besides, I was curious to learn what could possibly have led to such an about-face.

I replied:

Sure. When and where?

She responded almost immediately:

Tomorrow at ten? Usual place?

For all I knew our *usual* place might have closed down during the intervening two years, but I assumed she must know otherwise, so I typed:

Okay. See you then.

***

I couldn't afford to keep eating out, not even at the Gerbil and Oyster's prices, so on my way home, I called in at the local mini-market, which was just down the road from my flat.

When I'd first moved to the area, I'd thought the name of the shop, ERIC'S for EVERYTHING, was a bold claim for such a small establishment, but since then, I'd come to respect that claim. No matter what you might need, Eric had one somewhere. And, on the few occasions that he didn't have something, he could usually lay his hands on it within twenty-four hours.

Eric had a weird habit of waving to everyone who walked into the shop. You could always spot new customers because they looked a little nonplussed by this unusual ritual. Regulars, like myself, had come to embrace it.

"Hiya, Eric." I returned his wave.

Like everyone else, I called him Eric, but he'd once

confided in me that his real name was Jimmy. When I'd asked why he hadn't called the shop by that name, he'd explained that JIMMY'S for EVERYTHING didn't alliterate.

"Anything in particular you're looking for, Kat?"

"Just something for tea."

"You mean dinner, don't you?"

"Not where I come from." Up north, in Leeds, you have your dinner at midday, and your tea around five or six. Despite having lived in the capital for several years, I refused to bow to the pressure to call tea dinner. "What have you got that's quick and cheap?"

"Eggs are on offer."

"I had egg on toast for breakfast. What about microwave meals? Anything in particular you'd recommend?"

"The Mrs and I are partial to the lasagne."

I wasn't in the mood for lasagne, so I searched through his other offerings and eventually settled on a frozen chicken dinner, which if the photo on the packet was to be believed, would have fed a family of five. Based upon past experience, I thought that very unlikely.

"Anything else, Kat?"

"No, thanks."

He put the frozen meal and the bottle of diet cola through the till. "What about these? They're on special offer." He held up a packet of chocolate digestive biscuits — my favourites. "Two for one."

Damn the man. He knew it was an offer I couldn't refuse.

"Go on, then."

Back at my flat, I wasn't too surprised to discover that the chicken meal was barely enough to feed one. In fact, for a few moments there, I thought they'd forgotten to include the chicken, but then I found it underneath one of the potatoes.

Still hungry after finishing the microwave feast, I munched my way through several of the BOGOF chocolate digestives. They never failed to hit the spot.

I was just about to put my feet up, ready to enjoy an evening of mindless TV, when there was a knock at the door. It was the Widow Manning, accompanied by my least favourite canine.

"He was supposed to go out thirty minutes ago, Kat. Where were you?" she demanded.

"Sorry I—err—" If truth be told, I'd forgotten all about it. "I was just on the phone."

"You'd best hurry up." She handed me his lead. "Otherwise he'll do his stuff in here."

"But I haven't got my shoes—" Too late—the Widow Manning had disappeared in the direction of her flat. "Stay!" I wagged my finger at the lab, in the hope that would get the message across.

When I went in search of my trainers, I made the mistake of not closing the door behind me. When I returned, the dog was nowhere to be seen.

"The Brick! Where are you?" I went out onto the landing, but there was no sign of him there. Had he got fed up of waiting and taken the lift himself? Get a grip, Kat. How could he have called the lift?

So, where was he?

That's when I heard him. He was under the table, trying to get into my chocolate digestives, and had knocked one of the kitchen chairs over. Fortunately, I got to him before he managed to get any out of the packet. "Don't you know chocolate is bad for you?"

The Widow Manning's assessment proved to be accurate. Upon arriving at the park, The Brick spent the first five minutes emptying his bladder, and the next five minutes, doing the other.

What would aliens make of all this, I wondered. If the first thing they saw was a human picking up dog poop, they'd no doubt conclude that the dog was the master and the man its slave.

And they wouldn't be far wrong.

"Where's The Wall?" It was Graham and his dog, Miles.

"His name is The Brick."

"Sorry. How could I forget?"

"Do you have a tent in this park? How come you're always here?"

"I could ask you the same thing."

"You wouldn't like to adopt him, would you?" I gestured to The Brick who had wandered off down the park.

"No, thanks. I didn't even want the one I've got."

"What's wrong with Miles?"

"Nothing, but I'm not really a dog person."

"So how come you have him? Did you mistake him for a packet of fish fingers while you were doing the weekly shop?"

"Getting him was my fiancée's idea. Then, a few months before we were due to get married, she dumped me for a guy in her office. Apparently, he's allergic to dogs."

"It looks like we've both ended up with dogs we didn't

sign up for."

"What do you do when you aren't picking up dog poop? For work I mean?"

"Why do you want to know?"

"Jeez, Kat, are you always such hard work? I'm just making small talk."

"Sorry. I'm a private investigator."

"Always the joker." He laughed. "Are you ever serious?"

"I'm not joking. I really am a P.I."

"Let's see your business card, then."

"I'm waiting for them to be printed."

"Of course you are."

"Okay, then. What about you? What do you do?"

"What do you think I do?"

"Something in the city. You have that look about you."

"What look?"

"That, *I'm minted and you're not* look."

"I'm a lawyer, as it happens."

"What did I say? Minted."

"I work for an NGO, so not so minted." As he spoke, he seemed to be distracted by something behind me. "What are they doing down there?"

I followed his gaze and saw three boys, teenagers by the look of it, who appeared to be taunting The Brick.

"I'll have a word," Graham started towards them.

"Don't bother. I've got this."

As I got closer, I could see that the tallest of the three boys was poking the dog with a stick.

"Hey, you! Stop that!"

"What are you going to do about it?" The boy with the stick poked the dog again, but this time The Brick reacted.

"He bit me!" The boy screamed.

I grabbed the dog by the collar and attached his lead. "You shouldn't have been taunting him."

The boy had pulled up the sleeve of his jacket, and much to my relief, there were no visible wounds. The Brick must have just had a hold of his sleeve.

"I'm going to report him!" The boy screamed in my face.

"Go home, little boy, and take your friends with you."

"I'll get him put down," he shouted, as he and his buddies made their way to the park gates.

"Are you okay?" Graham said.

"Yeah. Horrible little sods."

"Did he bite the lad?"

"No, just his jacket, but to hear him scream, you'd have thought he'd taken his arm off."

"So, are you going to tell me what you do for a living or not?"

"I've already told you. It's not my fault if you don't believe me."

"Okay, let's say I believe you're a P.I. What cases are you working on at the moment?"

"I can't tell you. Client confidentiality and all that."

"How very convenient." He grinned.

"If you don't believe I'm a P.I, what do you think I do?"

"I would have had you down as working in a shop. Maybe a sandwich shop. You look like you know your way around a bacon cob."

"You got me. That's exactly what I do."

"Really?"

"No, of course not."

"How come your boyfriend doesn't take turns walking

the dog?"

"Is that your not so subtle way of trying to find out if I'm with someone?"

"Possibly."

"Not that it's any of your business, but I'm not."

"In that case, would you be open to the idea of having a drink with me sometime?"

"Why would I want to have a drink with someone who doesn't believe a word I say?"

"What if I said I believe you're a P.I?"

"Too late." I turned to the dog. "Come on, boy. It's time to get you back to the Widow Manning."

"Did you hear that?" I said to the dog on the walk back to my flat. "He asked me out." It was obvious that The Brick couldn't have cared less. He was far too focussed on getting back to the Widow Manning, where his dinner would be waiting for him. Despite the fact that I'd turned Graham down, it made a pleasant change to be asked out by someone who wasn't either married, ugly or the wrong side of fifty.

It had been a long time.

Back at the flat, I gave Sheila a call, and passed on the good news about my plans to keep on the agency. I'd expected her to be thrilled, but she was very subdued, and barely reacted to the news.

Chapter 6

I couldn't put it off any longer. My underwear drawer was practically empty, and I had precisely one clean t-shirt. I always used to do my own washing, but after the door broke on my last washing machine and flooded the kitchen, I swore never to buy another. These days, I preferred to avail myself of the full-service wash offered by Suds, the launderette across the road, next door to the greengrocer.

My plan was to sneak out of my flat so that the Widow Manning wouldn't hear me. Although she wasn't in the best of health, she wasn't exactly housebound either. She managed to get to bingo three or four times every week, so there was no reason why she couldn't take The Brick out occasionally. If I had to walk the dog and call in at the launderette, it would be mid-morning before I made it into the office. It might be my business now, but I couldn't just turn up at any old time of day. What kind of message would that send to potential clients?

I'd managed to squash all of my dirty washing into two giant black plastic sacks, and I was just about to leave the flat when someone knocked on the door. Crap! Had the Widow Manning anticipated my early morning manoeuvrings?

It wasn't her. Instead, standing there was a young boy, wearing a green blazer and grey trousers.

"Excuse me, Mrs. Have you got Rexy?"

"I think you must have the wrong flat."

"Someone told me you'd taken him in."

"Who's Rexy?"

"A dog. He used to belong to that man who sat on the

steps down the road."

"Do you mean The Brick?"

"That's what the man called him, but it's a silly name, so I always called him Rexy. The man used to let me take him for a walk."

Just then, as if on cue, the Widow Manning came out of her flat with the old lab at her feet.

"This young man reckons Walt used to let him take the dog for a walk."

"How do we know we can trust him?" The Widow Manning wasn't renowned for trusting anyone.

"Rexy!" the boy called. "Come here, Rexy!"

The dog hurried over to the boy.

"It looks like this young man was telling the truth," I said. "The dog even answers to the other name."

"Can I still take him for a walk?" The boy was stroking the excited dog.

"I don't see why not. How often did you used to take him out?"

"Most mornings before I went to school, and sometimes after school, depending on how much homework I had."

"That's fine by me." I looked over to the Widow Manning. "Unless you have any objections?"

She shrugged.

"That's settled, then. What's your name?"

"Luke Grimes."

"Are you Robbie's boy?"

"Yeah. I live over the greengrocers."

"And you're sure your parents are cool with this?"

"They don't mind as long as I'm not late for school, and I get my homework done."

"Okay then, that's settled. Off you go."

Luke and The Brick, or maybe I should call him Rexy now, made their way to the lift. This was a definite result for me. It meant I would only have to walk the dog when Luke couldn't do it.

***

"Hi, Kat." Elsie, who managed the launderette, always had a cigarette hanging out of the corner of her mouth, but it was never lit. "I was beginning to think you'd died or gone and bought yourself a new washing machine."

"I've been meaning to come over for the last week, but things have been a bit hectic." I held up the two black bags. "I've got twice the usual amount."

"No problem. Do you want to pick it up on your way home as usual?"

"Yes, please."

"That was a rum old business with Walt across the road, wasn't it? I heard someone threw him a tenner and the shock killed him."

"You're awful, Elsie."

"If I didn't laugh these days, I'd spend all of my time crying. Is it right you've taken on that old fleabag of his?"

"The Widow Manning took the dog in, and she browbeat me into agreeing to walk him occasionally. Mind you, Robbie's boy has just volunteered to take over most of the walking duties."

"Luke? He's a good lad, that one. Not like a lot of the youngsters these days. Some of them come in here, throwing the washing around. Mind you, they don't stick around once I show them this." She walked over to the corner of the room, and leaned down to pick up a baseball bat, which had been hidden behind one of the driers. "I call it Bruiser."

I didn't blame them for running away. I wouldn't have fancied going up against Elsie and Bruiser.

***

When I arrived at the office, Sheila was already at her desk and she didn't look very happy.

"Are you okay, Sheila?"

"There's something I have to tell you, Kat. I should have said something when you phoned last night, but I wanted to do it face to face."

"What's wrong?"

"I'm really sorry. If there was any other way —"

"What is it?"

"I have to give up this job."

"Why? If you're worried I won't be able to pay you, I've—"

"It isn't that. It's Don. I've been deluding myself. He's really poorly, and he isn't going to get better any time soon." She hesitated, and for a moment, I thought she was going to cry, but she managed to compose herself. "I'm really sorry to let you down like this. I know it's terrible timing."

"Don't worry your head about it. Don has to come first. Couldn't you just take a few weeks off, and see how it goes?"

"I appreciate the offer, Kat. It's very kind of you, but it wouldn't help. This could go on for ages."

"What will you do for money?"

"We've got Don's pension. It isn't a lot, but when you

add in the benefits we'll be entitled to, we should just about get by."

"When do you want to leave?"

"Now if that's okay with you? I just came in to clear out my stuff."

"Of course it's okay."

It didn't take her long to gather her things together; twenty minutes later, she was ready to leave.

"Take care, Sheila." I gave her a hug. "If you ever need anything, you know where to find me."

"Thanks, Kat. I know you're going to make a success of the business. If it hadn't been for you, this place would have gone to the wall ages ago."

This wasn't exactly the start that I'd been hoping for. There was no way I could run the business by myself. I needed someone to answer the phone to potential customers, and to do research. Where was I supposed to find someone who would be prepared to work for peanuts, be willing to take a chance on a new business, and who was available to start immediately? Sonya was one possibility, but she'd only be able to work part-time, and I needed someone full-time.

That's when I remembered the strange young man who had handed me his CV in the school canteen. Where had I put it?

I eventually found it, screwed up at the bottom of my bag, and I gave him a call.

"Is that — err — Zero?"

"Yeah, who's this?"

"Kat Royle. You gave me your CV yesterday."

"I've given a lot of people my CV."

"I was the one who asked if you like broccoli."

"Oh yeah." He laughed. "I remember you. Have you got something for me?"

"Possibly. You said you were good with computers and numbers, does that mean you can do bookkeeping?"

"Piece of cake. Profit and loss, balance sheet, management accounts — what do you need?"

"I don't know, but probably some of those. What's your telephone manner like?"

"You tell me. You're talking to me on it."

"I guess I am. Look, I'm not sure if what I have in mind would be suitable for you or not. Why don't we meet for coffee and we can talk about it?"

"Okay. When and where?"

"What are you doing right now?"

"Handing out more CVs."

"Do you know Joe's Café? It's close to the Sidings Business Centre."

"I'll find it. I can be there in half an hour."

"Okay. I'll see you there."

***

"Hi, Kat. How's it rolling?" Joe was the owner of the café. A rotund man in his early fifties, he was a walking advert for his own food.

"Alright thanks, Joe."

"I hear that boss of yours met a sticky end. You didn't do it, did you?"

"Innocent."

"I wouldn't have blamed you if you had. Roy always was a tosser. What can I get you?"

"I'll have a mocha with double cream and a marshmallow."

"You'll have a filter coffee and like it."

"Okay. Give me one of those gingerbread men too, would you?"

"Gingerbread *person* if you don't mind. Haven't you heard they're gender neutral now?"

"Is that an excuse to make them smaller?"

"Probably."

When Zero arrived ten minutes later, I handed him a fiver, and told him to get himself a drink.

"Like I said on the phone, there's a possibility I may have something for you."

"Cool. What do you have in mind?"

"Before I start, I ought to point out that I'm not going to be able to pay much to begin with. It'll be minimum wage initially, but if things work out, that should increase pretty quickly."

"I'm cool with that. What is it you do, exactly?"

"I'm a private investigator."

"Really? Sweet. What would I be doing?"

"I'll be spending a lot of time out of the office. I need someone who can field calls from clients and potential clients while I'm out."

"No problem."

"Also, as I mentioned before, I'll need someone to do the bookkeeping."

"Okay."

"On top of that, it'll be pretty much anything I throw at you."

"Sounds good to me. When do I start?"

"Now would be as good a time as any. Can you manage that?"

"Sure."

"Great. Drink up, we'll go to the office and I'll show you your desk. By the way, what do I call you? People don't really call you Zero, do they?"

"Why wouldn't they? That's my name."

If Zero was unimpressed by my offices, he managed to hide it well.

"That will be yours." I pointed to the desk which until a couple of hours earlier had belonged to Sheila.

"Cool." He spun around on the chair. "What do I call you? Boss?"

"Kat will do just fine. I have to go out in a few minutes. If anyone calls, you should answer the phone as R.K. Investigations. If you need to talk to me about anything, just give me a call. You have my number, don't you?"

"Yeah, it's on my mobile. What else do you want me to do?"

"I'd like you to find out exactly what open cases my boss was working on."

"I thought you were the boss?"

"Sorry, I probably should have explained."

I gave Zero the Cliff Notes version of what had happened to Roy.

"So I guess that means you've only just taken over the business?"

"That's right. Does that change your mind about wanting to take the job?"

"No way. I like a challenge."

"That's probably just as well. Anyway, I'd better get

going."

"Before you do, where will I find the info on the cases? Is it on here?" He pointed to the computer.

"I wish. The computer was only ever used to send out letters and bills. All the cases are on paper in that filing cabinet behind you."

"That's crazy."

"It's just how Roy worked. He was stuck in the seventies. You only had to look at the way he dressed to know that."

"What about the accounts? Are they on computer?"

"No, they're all paper-based too. Roy took the books home with him on Saturday. I'll have to try to get those back from his house if I can."

Chapter 7

The *usual place*, as Christine had referred to it, was Pointers coffee shop, just off Denmark Street. For some reason, I was feeling ridiculously nervous about seeing her again after all this time. Although I would never have called us BFFs (I wouldn't call anyone a BFF because I'm not thirteen), we had once been good friends.

I arrived a few minutes early and took a seat by the window, so I could keep a lookout for her. We spotted one another at pretty much the same time. Her hair was longer than the last time I'd seen her, and if I wasn't mistaken, she'd coloured it a little. Christine had always been the fashion conscious one, and that obviously hadn't changed. She looked fabulous.

We hugged a very awkward hug.

"Great to see you again, Kat. Thanks for agreeing to meet me."

"No problem. How have you been keeping?"

"Oh, you know."

I didn't, but based on the tone of her voice, I guessed the answer was probably: *not great*.

Once we had our drinks, we found a table at the back of the shop.

"I was surprised to hear from you." I took a sip of the over-priced Americano.

"I've been trying to find the courage to contact you for a couple of weeks."

"That's silly."

"Is it, though? I told you I didn't ever want to see you again."

"And don't forget, you said that I was dead to you." I

grinned.

"I did say that, didn't I?" She at least had the good grace to blush. "You must have thought I was a right idiot."

"Yeah, I did."

"I'm really sorry." She was threading the spoon back and forth through her fingers. "About everything."

"Forget it. We all say stupid things."

"Like when you said you were going to run away to join the circus?"

"Did I say that?"

"Yes, but then you were a little drunk at the time. Where are you living now?"

"In Lewford."

"Are you with anyone?"

"No, it's just me and the cockroaches."

"It's not as bad as that, is it?"

"Not quite. What about you? Where do you live now?"

"Purley."

"Flat?"

"No, we've got a small terraced house."

"Nice."

"Are you still doing the private investigation stuff?"

"Yeah, for the moment at least."

"You're probably wondering why I contacted you out of the blue."

"I figured you'd get around to telling me when you were ready."

"It's Ralph."

"I thought it might be."

"If you want to say you told me so, I wouldn't blame you."

"What's he done?"

"We got married last year."

"What? Get out of here."

She held up her left hand, and for the first time, I noticed the wedding ring. "Where was my invitation?"

"I — err — I'm really — "

"It's okay. I'm only kidding. You did me a favour. I hate weddings, and at least I didn't have to fork out for a present."

"I'm sorry I didn't believe you when you told me that Ralph was cheating on me. I should never have accused you of being jealous."

"What changed your mind?"

"I think he's cheating on me now."

"What makes you think that?"

"It's a lot of little things. He's been acting really weird for about a month. Normally, he gets home at the same time every day, but recently he's been making all kinds of excuses for getting home late. And even when he is home, he barely has two words to say to me. It's as though he's there, but he's not, if you know what I mean?"

"Have you confronted him about the way he's been acting?"

"Yes, but he said it was all in my imagination. That's why I contacted you. I'm hoping you'll be able to find out what's going on."

"I'm not sure that's a good idea."

"Please, Kat. I know I treated you badly, but I really need this. I've got a good job now, so I can pay you."

"It's not that. Ralph knows me, remember. Surveillance is difficult enough when the target isn't likely to recognise you."

"He only met you a couple of times, and besides, you've

changed since then."

"Got older, you mean?"

"No. Your hair is much shorter. It suits you, by the way."

"Thanks."

"And you're slimmer too. Have you been working out?"

"Not really. I just can't afford to eat a lot of the time."

"Are you still working at the same place?"

"Yes and no. I'm still at R.K. Investigations, but I run the business now."

"Since when?"

"Since a couple of days ago when the previous owner was murdered."

"That's what I like about you, Kat." She laughed. "You always did have a sense of humour."

"Actually, I'm not joking. He really was murdered."

"Oh? I'm sorry. Will you do this for me, Kat? Please."

"Do you have any idea who Ralph is cheating with?"

"I've got a pretty good idea who it is. I'm almost certain it's the woman he works with. She's new, and it was shortly after she started working there that he changed. I wish I'd listened to you. I could have saved myself all this grief."

"Where does he work?"

"At a betting shop in Greenwich: BetMore, do you know it?"

"Not offhand, but I live just up the road, so it shouldn't take much finding."

"Will you take the case, Kat? Please."

"Sure, why not?"

Back at the office, Zero's desk was surrounded by a sea of cardboard box files. Meanwhile, the man himself was busy tapping away at the keyboard.

"Don't worry if you haven't managed to make any sense of it yet." I sat on the edge of his desk. "I should have some time to go through it with you tomorrow."

"There's no need. It's almost done."

"Already?"

"There wasn't much to go through. The only live cases I could find were those you're working on. It doesn't appear that your boss was working on anything. In fact, the last case assigned to him was closed three months ago. The only other cases are those assigned to someone called West."

"That's Westy."

"It looks like he's worked on a few cases over the last year, but they all appear to be closed too."

"That can't be right. Westy must have been working on something recently because he came around here chasing his money."

"Well, if he is, the case file isn't in that filing cabinet."

"Are you sure about all of this?"

"One hundred percent, but you're welcome to double-check my findings."

"You're telling me that Roy hasn't worked on any cases in the last three months?"

"Correct."

"So, if I understand you correctly, the only money coming into the business was from the cases I was working on?"

"That's right. And maybe a few that Westy was working on."

"Unbelievable! He was always giving me a hard time for not pulling my weight." I laughed, but I actually felt like crying. "I'll kill him."

"It seems someone beat you to that. Having seen this mess, I'm really concerned about the accounts. Do you have any idea what the balance sheet looks like?"

"I wouldn't know one if someone smacked me in the face with it."

"You need to get hold of the books as soon as possible. I'm worried this business could be insolvent."

"I'm guessing that's not a good thing."

"You'd be right about that."

"If it is — err — ?"

"Insolvent."

"What can I do about it?"

"You need to bring in more work and cash, fast."

"I can't believe you got all that done so quickly."

"It wasn't difficult. This is a fairly simple business. I've also put the live cases into an online case management system."

"How did you manage to do that? Doesn't it cost money for the software?"

"I used an open-source application. It was free. I've also printed out a list of the open cases." He leaned back and grabbed a sheet of A4 paper from the printer. "Fulton & Associates, Marston, and Premax. That's it."

"You can close the Marston case. I persuaded her she didn't need our services."

"Why would you do that?"

"It seemed like the right thing to do at the time. She's

going to drop in and pay us for the time we've already spent on the case. Also, you can add one more case to that list: Christine Mather."

He began to tap on the keyboard again. "What's the case about?"

"Suspected infidelity."

"Got it. Any others?"

"I'm going to be investigating Roy's murder for his daughter, Anne."

"Okay."

"We won't be getting paid for that one, though."

"Can you afford to do pro bono work?"

"Probably not, but I'm not going to charge Anne for trying to find her father's murderer."

"You're the boss. What this business really needs is some kind of online presence. How do you expect anyone to even know it's here?"

"That's what Half-An-Ear said."

"Who's Half-An-Ear?"

"Vic the printer. He said I needed to sort out my social media, but I wouldn't know where to start. And besides, I can't afford it."

"I can sort all of that out for you—no problem."

"What about the cost?"

"It won't cost you a penny."

"Are you sure?"

"Piece of cake. I can have it done by this time tomorrow."

"I'm starting to like you, even if you do have a weird name."

Just then, the door flew open and in walked Westy. He

had the distinction of being the only man I knew with a worse dress sense than Roy.

"I want my money!" His pig breath was as bad as ever.

"You can't just come bursting in here like this, Westy."

"I can when you owe me money."

"What are you talking about? I don't owe you a penny."

"A little bird told me that you'd taken over Roy's business."

"I have. So what?"

"Then you've taken over his debts too."

"There are no open cases assigned to you," Zero chipped in.

"Who's this idiot?" Westy glared at Zero.

"He's my new assistant. He's just brought the case management system up to date, and you heard what he said: There are no cases assigned to you."

"I don't care about your fancy systems. I've been working a case for Roy. I'm owed money and I expect to get it."

"What have you been working on?"

"None of your business."

"It is my business if you expect me to pay you for it."

"Get me the money, and I'll hand over the file."

"Hand over the file and I'll think about it."

"No chance. Money first."

"How much did Roy owe you?"

"A grand."

"Cobblers. No way Roy would have paid you a grand."

"It's a grand!"

"I don't have that kind of money."

"You'd better find it by the end of the week or you'll be sorry."

"Is that a threat?"

"You'll find out." And with that, he made for the door.

"Nice to see you too, Westy."

"Shouldn't you be more worried about that guy?" Zero said, once Westy had left.

"Probably."

***

Given the dire state of the business, all my attention should have been focussed on the three paying cases I had on the books, but I'd made a promise to Anne that I'd try to find out who'd murdered her father, and I intended to keep that promise.

My relationship with the local police wasn't the best. During the time I'd been working for Roy, I'd had a number of run-ins with them, and I'd ended up in a cell twice. Only for a few hours both times, and nothing that resulted in my being charged with anything. Fortunately for me, there wasn't a law against being a pain in their backside, otherwise I would have done serious jail time.

I did still have one friendly contact on the force, though. Bruce Layne was an old-school copper who was a few years away from retirement. He didn't have much time for modern policing methods or for any of his bosses. He and I had met a couple of years earlier when I'd been working on a case where a lovely old lady had been conned out of most of her life savings. I'd been struck by the compassion he'd shown to her; he'd definitely gone above and beyond. The money was never recovered, and Enid had died a few months later. Bruce and I had been amongst the few mourners at her funeral.

I gave him a call.

"Hey, Batman. How's it going?"

"That never gets old. What's up, Kat?"

"I was just thinking that I hadn't seen you for a long time."

"What you really mean is that you want something."

"Why would you say that?"

"Because you always do."

"How about five o'clock in The Orchard?"

"Are the drinks on you?"

"Of course."

"Okay, I'll see you there."

Chapter 8

"I'm going out, Zero," I said.

"Before you go, can I have your phone for a minute?"

"Why?"

"I want to install an app on it."

"Nothing too high tech, I hope." I handed him my phone anyway.

"How long have you had this thing?" He grinned.

"What's wrong with it?"

"I didn't think they still made these."

"It does everything I need."

He played around with it for a couple of minutes, and then beckoned me to take a look. "I've installed TimeLogMaster."

"What does that do?"

"It'll record how much time you spend on each case."

"I do that already."

"How?"

"I estimate it at the end of each day."

"Very scientific." He pointed to the screen. "I've synchronised this with your case management system. When you start working, you select the appropriate case and press the green button. When you've finished, you press the red button."

"Is that all I have to do?"

"Yeah. It will automatically log all your time to the appropriate case. That way you know how much to bill the customer. More importantly, you'll be able to keep tabs on whether you've made a profit or a loss on each case." He handed back the phone. "Give it a go."

"What do I do?"

"What are you working on at the moment?"

"I'm going to check out Mike Dale's house."

"Which case is that?"

"Fulton."

"You need to select that case and press the green button."

"Shouldn't I do that when I arrive there?"

"No. You should be logging every minute from the moment you step out of this office."

"Fair enough." I selected the Fulton case from the menu, and pressed the green button.

"Don't forget to press the red button when you get back here."

"Actually, I probably won't be back this afternoon because I'm working undercover on the Premax case tonight."

"Just make sure you update the app when you finish on one case and start on the other."

"I'll do my best to remember. I'm not sure what time I'll get in tomorrow."

"No problem. I've got plenty to be working on. With a bit of luck, your social media presence should be sorted out by this time tomorrow. I'll set you up on Facebook, Twitter and Instagram to start with."

"Won't it be a lot of work to keep all those updated?"

"No, trust me. And, besides, I'll look after all the routine stuff."

"Okay. I'd better be making tracks. Give me a call if anything urgent crops up."

"Will do, and don't forget to use TimeLogMaster."

"Okay."

I was feeling really pleased with my decision to take on

Zero. Within the space of a couple of days, he'd sorted out my case management system, and if he was to be believed, I'd soon be the queen of social media.

***

Mike Dale lived in a mews house in Knightsbridge. It wasn't a rental—according to the Land Registry, he owned the property outright. Not even a mortgage. It appeared that he'd lived in the house for just over three years. At today's prices, you'd get very little change out of two million.

I'd been given to believe that Mike Dale wasn't currently in a relationship, but while studying the property from across the road, I spotted someone in one of the downstairs rooms. I only caught a quick glimpse of them, but it appeared to be a woman in her forties.

I rang the doorbell and waited.

"Yes?" The woman opened the door just wide enough to peek out.

"Is this Mike Dale's house?"

"It is. I'm his housekeeper."

"My name is Kat Royle. I've been hired by Mr Dale's business partner, Ted Fulton, to try to locate Mr Dale. Do you happen to know where he is?"

She opened the door a little wider. "No, he didn't tell me he was going away."

"Did he take any clothes with him?"

"No, his cases are still in the spare bedroom. I checked as soon as he didn't come home."

"Would it be possible for me to come in and ask you a few questions?" I glanced up. "Please, it's starting to rain out here."

"I suppose so." She moved to one side, so I could step into the hallway.

"Would you like something to drink?"

"A cup of tea would be nice."

While making the tea, Rhian took the opportunity to tell me her life story. Originally from Wales, she'd been working in London for over ten years. This was her third housekeeping position, and judging by the way she talked about it, her favourite so far.

"What kind of boss is Mr Dale?"

"Very good compared to some of the people I've worked for. He's fair, very friendly and he never talks down to me."

"Does he normally tell you when he's decided to go away somewhere?"

"Yes, even if it's just for a long weekend."

"Had you noticed any kind of change in him in the days before he disappeared?"

"No, he was pretty much the same as usual." She took a sip of her tea.

"No change to his routine? Nothing else unusual?"

"No." She hesitated. "Except for the break-in, but that happened afterwards."

"When?"

"The day after he left."

"What did they take?"

"Nothing. I wouldn't have known they'd been inside the house if it hadn't been for the forced window. I found it when I arrived the next morning."

"It's strange that they didn't take anything."

"The police reckon they must have been spooked by

something and made a run for it."

"What about Mr Dale's friends? Did he have many?"

"None that came around here."

"No one?"

"Not that I saw. Apart from Lisa of course."

"Lisa?"

"I assumed you knew about her. She and Mr Dale were in a relationship for a while."

"Did she move in with him?"

"Not exactly, but she did quite often spend the night here, and he regularly stayed at her place."

"What happened to the relationship? Do you know?"

"Not really. They just stopped seeing one another."

"You wouldn't happen to have her address, would you?"

"No. I do have her phone number, though. Would you like it?"

"Yes, please. That would be great." I gave her one of my new business cards that I'd collected from Vic earlier. "Would you call me if you think of anything else? Anything at all."

"Okay."

***

The Orchard was an old-style boozer. No designer beers to be found here, and the only food served was crisps, nuts and pork scratchings.

"We don't see you in here much these days, Kat." Roly the landlord hadn't trimmed his beard this side of the millennium.

"I was in last Wednesday."

"Were you? That's when I was having my boil lanced."

"Too much information, Roly."

"At least I can sit down now."

"Way too much."

"What are you drinking?"

"Just a lime and lemon."

"You haven't gone and got yourself a car, have you?"

"No. I can't have a drink because I'm working tonight."

"I see that boss of yours got himself murdered. My money was on you doing it."

"Cheers, buddy. It wasn't me who did it, but I am trying to find out who did. When was the last time you saw him?"

"He came in here most Fridays, and sometimes on a Saturday lunchtime if he'd had a few bets."

"Was he ever with anyone?"

"Not usually." Roly handed me the drink. "He was a bit of a loner, like you." He glanced over at the door. "Watch out, Batman's here!"

Bruce Layne rolled his eyes at Roly, and then greeted me with the obligatory air kiss.

"I'll get Bruce's drink." I handed Roly a fiver.

Once Bruce had his beer, he and I found a quiet table in the corner.

"Thanks for agreeing to meet me, Bruce."

"It's not like I had anything better to do. I bet I can guess what it's about."

"Roy."

"That's what I figured. I didn't think you could stand the guy?"

"We weren't exactly best buddies, but I'm doing this for his daughter, Anne. She's pretty upset, as you can imagine."

"I believe she was the one who found him?"

"Yeah. Poor girl."

"My deepest sympathies go out to the girl, but she should leave the investigation to the professionals."

"Come on, Bruce. Your lot aren't interested. They're trying to make out it was a burglary gone wrong. That's utter nonsense."

"Who says?"

"I do, and so does Anne. Why would they leave without taking the rest of his Rolexes?"

"Maybe the burglar panicked?"

"I still don't buy it. Roy had made a lot of enemies over the years. Some really nasty people."

"The kind of people you're talking about wouldn't have killed him in his own home. They'd have knocked him off down a dark alley somewhere. This wasn't a professional hit, Kat. All the indications are that Roy disturbed a burglar who panicked, grabbed a knife and struck out."

"How did the burglar get in? Anne told me that the door was locked when she arrived. It wasn't damaged and there were no broken windows."

"Maybe the guy was already in the house when Roy got back. Roy might have forgotten to lock the door when he went out. That man did like his drink."

"So that's it, is it? That's all you're going to do?"

"It isn't up to me, Kat. It's not my case."

"Whose is it?"

"Menzies'."

"I met him at my office. Do you think he'd talk to me?"

He laughed. "Not a prayer."

"So what can I do?"

"Find the real murderer."

Oh crap. I'd just realised that I hadn't clocked off the Fulton case when I left Dale's house. This app thing was going to take a lot of getting used to.

I had hoped to get a few hours' kip before reporting for duty at Premax, but my meeting with Bruce had put paid to that idea.

Chapter 9

Premax Acoustics was based on the Cottram Industrial Park in Islington. The company manufactured high quality micro-speakers, which were rebranded and sold by some of the biggest names in audio. Over the previous six months, someone had been stealing those speakers in alarmingly large numbers. The thefts had all happened at night during which time the offices and factory were cleaned by contract cleaners.

Kevin Lockhart, the M.D, had convinced the owner of the contract cleaning company to let me join the cleaning team assigned to Premax. He'd met with little resistance because a refusal would have resulted in Premax cancelling the lucrative contract. So far, I'd completed one shift undercover at the plant, but I'd seen nothing to raise any suspicions.

Before meeting up with the cleaning crew, I called Kevin Lockhart.

"Kat? I heard about Roy, and I was beginning to think I'd have to look for someone else to take over the investigation."

"That won't be necessary. I'm sorry I've missed a couple of shifts, but as you can imagine, things went a bit pear-shaped after what happened to Roy."

"Understandably. What's going to happen to the agency?"

"I've taken it over. Things will continue as before."

"We really need to get to the bottom of these thefts once and for all."

"I know. Hopefully, I'll have more luck tonight."

Zero would have been proud of me because I'd remembered to set TimeLogMaster running on the Premax case.

A minibus collected me from outside London Bridge station. I was the last of the cleaning crew to be collected, and the only seats free were those at the very rear of the bus. No one wanted to sit there because the rear seats were raised, which meant there was less headroom.

None of the other cleaners, including Gillian the supervisor, were aware that I was a 'plant'. They no doubt viewed me as something of a liability because my pace had been way slower than what was expected. I also had an annoying habit of going missing, as I made frequent excursions to different areas of the building.

"Hey, Flash," Gillian shouted. She'd given me the nickname on my first night in the job. "I thought you must have thrown in the towel when you didn't show up yesterday or the day before."

"Nah. I've had a bad cold."

"A *cold*?" Tina scoffed. She was Gillian's unofficial second-in-command. "I wish I could afford to take time off with a runny nose. I managed to get here with a sprained ankle once, didn't I, Gill?"

"Yeah. These youngsters just don't want work."

The temptation to answer back was very strong, but my alter ego, Rebecca, was too meek to do anything like that.

"Just don't keep going walkabout tonight or I'll have to file a report on you."

"Sorry. It's just my weak bladder."

"Jeez." Tina scoffed. "This poor little flower is falling apart."

Security at the factory was very tight. Surrounded by a fifteen-foot tall fence, the only access was through a gatehouse that was manned twenty-four seven.

After the minibus had pulled up at the gate, the driver allowed the security guard to get onboard so that he could scan the tags we were required to wear at all times. Once he was satisfied, he stepped down from the minibus, and waved us through. The main doors were locked at seven o'clock, so we had to enter via the fire exit at the rear of the building, adjacent to the loading bay.

Once inside, each cleaner made their way to the area designated to them. Access around the building was controlled by the same ID tags that had been used to identify us at the gatehouse. Fortunately, each cleaner worked alone, which gave me a certain amount of freedom. Even so, I was conscious that Gillian would spend all night checking on us, and I was sure that I'd be getting more than my fair share of her attention.

I was hoping that I might spot someone inside the building who shouldn't have been there, but so far, the only people I'd seen had been the other cleaners. Could one of them be involved in the thefts? I didn't see how because we all arrived and left together. It's not like they could have simply walked out of the factory with a box of speakers under their arm. And even if they had, they wouldn't have got through the gates.

"Daydreaming again, Flash?" Gillian had a knack for sneaking up on me.

"Sorry." I began to empty the bins.

"I don't understand why you took this job. You're

clearly not cut out for it. What job did you do before this one?"

"I worked in a shop."

"Which one?"

"You wouldn't know it. A greengrocer in Lewford."

"I hope you knew your onions better than you know your mops." She laughed at what I assumed was supposed to be a joke.

For the rest of the night, I did the bare minimum of cleaning, in-between checking out the rest of the building, in the hope that I might see someone or something suspicious.

I didn't. And by the time we were collected by the same minibus, at four o'clock in the morning, I was dead on my feet.

At least I'd be able to have a lie-in.

***

Someone was knocking at my door.

"You can't be serious!" I rolled over, and grabbed my phone from the bedside cabinet. It was seven-thirty! Who could that be at this time of the morning? Whoever it was would be sorry.

I threw on some jeans and the t-shirt I'd worn the previous day, and then started for the door.

Not quickly enough, apparently, because there was another knock.

I pulled open the door to find the Widow Manning standing there. "What?"

"He needs to go out." She gestured to the lab.

"I thought Luke was going to walk him?"

"He sent word last night that he has a school trip today. He had to go in early."

"Can't you take him this once? I was working last night."

"I would but my varicose veins are giving me gyp." She handed me the lead. "You'd better look sharp because he's been making some awful smells."

Great!

I grabbed my shoes and headed for the lift. It wasn't until I was stuck in that confined space with a flatulent dog that I realised how slowly those lifts travelled. By the time we reached ground level, I was ready to claw the doors open.

As soon as we arrived at the park, the dog did his stuff. I was genuinely worried that the small plastic bags might not be up to the task; whoever had designed them obviously hadn't accounted for this volume of output.

While I was posting the revolting package into the bin, the dog wandered off down the park. "Hey, Rexy, don't go too far!"

"Who's Rexy?"

When I turned around, Graham and his dog were standing there.

"You're beginning to look like a stalker."

"You didn't answer my question. Who's Rexy?"

"The dog, of course. Who else would I be shouting at?"

"The black lab? I thought he was called The Brick?"

"He was. He still is, I suppose."

"What did he do, change his name by deed poll?"

"It's complicated."

"You've been having a laugh at my expense, haven't

you? He never was called The Brick, was he? You must have thought I was a right mug to fall for that."

"Do you want to hear the explanation or not?"

"Go on. I'm listening."

"The dog's official name *is* The Brick. I discovered yesterday that the young lad from the greengrocer used to walk him for Walt. Luke, that's the kid, decided to call him Rexy. I'm surprised you haven't seen the two of them in here."

"Maybe I have, but they're unlikely to have registered on my radar. You, on the other hand, made an immediate impression."

"Am I supposed to be flattered by that?"

"If you like. By the way, have you decided where we're going?"

"Going when?"

"For that drink you promised to have with me."

"I seem to recall I turned you down flat."

"Yeah, but I could tell you didn't mean it."

"A mind reader, are you?"

"Come on, Kat. What harm can one little drink do?"

"I'm way too busy at the moment. I was working until four this morning."

"Doing what?"

"I've told you what I do for a living. If it wasn't for Rexy here, I'd still be in bed." I glanced around. "Where did he go?"

There was no sign of the lab.

"He can't have gone far." Graham unclipped the lead from his dog's collar. "Go find him, boy!"

Miles headed down the park at a rate of knots, with Graham and me in hot pursuit.

"The Widow Manning will kill me if anything has happened to him."

"Don't worry. Miles will find him."

As Miles reached the far edge of the park, he suddenly veered to the right, towards a clump of bushes close to the railings. Moments after he'd disappeared from view, he began to bark loudly.

Much to my relief, when we caught up with Miles, he was standing next to Rexy who was flat out, seemingly on the verge of sleep.

"You silly dog." I clipped on his lead. "Don't ever do that again."

"So?" Graham had a stupid grin on his face. "Now that I've helped to find your dog, are you going to change your mind about that drink?"

"You didn't find him. Miles did."

"Do I have to beg?"

"It couldn't do any harm."

"Would you please go for a drink with me, Kat? Pretty please?"

"I'll think about it when things quieten down at work."

"When will that be?"

I shrugged, and then started back up the park with Rexy in tow.

***

"I thought you said you'd be late in today." Zero looked up from the computer.

"That was the plan, but the dog had other ideas."

"You have a dog?"

"He's not really mine. Not all of him, anyway."

"Who owns the rest of him?"

"The Widow Manning and Luke."

"That sounds like some kind of superhero mashup. I must admit, you don't strike me as a dog person."

"What makes you say that?"

"I don't know. You seem like more of a *kat* person." He laughed.

"I do the jokes in this office. Were there any calls this morning?"

"Yeah. Kevin Lockhart called about ten minutes ago. He wants you to ring him as soon as possible."

"Okay." I started towards my office.

"Your Facebook account is up and running by the way."

"You'll have to show me later."

"Kevin, it's Kat. I have a message to call you."

"Were you at the factory last night?"

"Yeah, but I didn't see anything out of the ordinary."

"That's rather unfortunate because we lost two more boxes of speakers last night."

"I don't get it. What about the CCTV? Have you checked that?"

"I did that earlier. There's nothing to see."

"I'm sorry, Kevin. I don't know what to tell you."

"I'm paying for results, Kat. I'm prepared to give you one more try, but if it happens again, I'll have to bring someone else in."

"Fair enough."

"Do you want to see your Facebook page?" Zero asked when I went through to the outer office.

"Later, maybe. I've just discovered I'm going to have to

work again tonight."

"I thought you worked last night?"

"I did."

"When will you sleep?"

"Your guess is as good as mine."

"I assume this is the Premax case?"

"Yeah, it seems like I messed up last night. The thieves managed to steal more speakers right from under my nose."

"What about CCTV? They must have it installed, don't they?"

"Yeah, but it didn't pick anything up."

"Are you sure?"

"I'm just going on what Kevin Lockhart told me. I haven't actually seen it myself."

"Why don't I take a look at it? I might spot something they've missed."

"I'd have to contact the MD to see if he'd be okay with you going into the factory."

"There's no need for that. I can check it from here."

"How are you going to do that? You'd need passwords and stuff, wouldn't you?"

"How very naïve you are." He grinned.

Chapter 10

I had no idea how Zero intended to access Premax's CCTV, and it was probably just as well that I didn't know.

Anne had been in touch to confirm that Roy's funeral would be on Tuesday next week. I'd said I'd be there, and I'd contacted Sheila who said she'd also attend, provided she could get someone to stay with Don for a couple of hours. While I had Anne on the phone, I asked if the police had released Roy's house yet.

"Yeah, they called me last night to say they'd finished with it."

"Is it okay for me to take a look around there?"

"Sure. Do you need me to be there?"

"Not unless you particularly want to be."

"I'd rather not. You'll find a key under the urn in the back garden."

"Okay. While I'm there, I'm going to see if I can find the accounts books. Your dad took them with him on Saturday. Is that okay with you?"

"Of course. They belong to the business, and that's yours now."

"Okay, thanks."

***

Roy had lived in a three-bed semi, which was a five-minute walk from Upney tube station. I found the back door key underneath the ugly urn next to the shed, just as Anne had said it would be. Inside, the house was cold. It was possible Anne had turned the central heating down, but it was just as likely that Roy had lived there with it like that. He hated to spend money on anything apart from cigars and his precious Rolexes. He probably hadn't spent much time at the house, anyway. I wasn't sure what exactly I was looking for, but I did find plenty of booze; there were enough empty bottles to fill a skip.

I'd just finished looking around the living room when someone tapped on the window. An old woman wagged a bony finger at me, and mouthed something about the police. I gestured to the back of the house, and then went through the kitchen to meet her at the door.

"I've called the police," she said. "They'll be here in a minute."

"I have permission to be here."

"From who? Roy is dead."

"From his daughter, Anne. I'm Kat Royle. I used to work for Roy."

"Oh. That's alright, then."

"I wish you'd talked to me before you called the police."

"I haven't actually called them." She grinned, and almost lost her top denture. "I only said that to scare you off. I'm Maureen but everyone calls me Mo."

"Do you live next door, Mo?"

"Yeah, the house adjoining. Nasty business with Roy. He could be a funny bugger, but he didn't deserve to go like that. I always figured he'd drink himself to death."

"He drank a lot, then?"

"You must have seen the bottles. He wasn't a lot of bother though. He kept himself to himself."

"What about visitors? Did he have many, do you know?"

"Not many that I saw. Occasionally, he'd bring some guys back from the boozer, and they'd carry on drinking here. Thankfully, that didn't happen too often."

"Did he have a local?"

"The Feathers. It's at the end of the road."

"What about lady friends?"

"Roy? Nah, who'd want to go with him?" She seemed to catch herself. "Sorry, I shouldn't speak ill of the dead."

"That's okay. I worked for Roy, but we weren't what you might call close."

"Does that bloke with the sideburns work with you, too?"

"What bloke?"

"He was here yesterday, sniffing around outside. He took off when he saw me."

"Whoever he is, he doesn't work with me. Sideburns, you say?"

"Yeah, big bushy ones."

"How old was he?"

"I'm not very good with ages. Older than you, but not as old as Roy."

"Will you do me a favour, Mo? If you see him or anyone else around here, would you give me a call on this number?" I handed her my card. "If I'm not in, there should be someone to take a message."

"No problem. Come around for a cuppa later if you like."

"Thanks."

I found the experience of looking around Roy's house quite depressing. Two out of the three bedrooms were full of old furniture and general junk. His bedroom hadn't seen a vacuum cleaner or a duster for several years, and the bedsheets looked as though they hadn't been changed for weeks if not months. On his bedside cabinet, there were two framed photographs, both of his daughter: One of Anne as a young child — maybe seven or eight years old, the other of her as an adult. Roy had never been one to talk about his personal life. Nor had he ever shown any interest in either mine or Sheila's lives outside of work. His other Rolex watches were still inside the unlocked cabinet.

Two hours later, despite having searched every nook and cranny, I'd found no clues that might lead me to his murderer. I hadn't even found the accounts books.

***

While I was in the area, I decided to check out the Feathers public house. It was unusual to find an old-fashioned boozer located on a housing estate these days. Most of them had been converted into mini-supermarkets run by one of the big three chains. If the number of customers inside today was typical, the Feathers' days had to be numbered too.

An elderly couple were seated at a table close to the fireplace. The woman was knitting; the man appeared to be asleep. On a stool at the bar was a middle-aged man, wearing a trilby and sucking on an electronic cigarette.

"Hello, young lady." The jolly grey giant behind the bar seemed genuinely pleased to see me. Perhaps he would have been just as pleased to see any customer come through the door. "What can I get for you?"

"Just a cola, please."

"Diet?"

"Nah, I'll take it straight."

"Coming right up. Don't think I've seen you around these parts before. Have you just moved to the area?"

"No. I live in Lewford."

"Are you lost?" He grinned.

"I used to work for Roy King who lived up the road. Did you know him?"

The man in the trilby spoke for the first time, "Don't mention Roy to Lenny. He was his best customer. This place will probably go broke now Roy's gone."

"Watch your mouth, Terry. This lady is a friend of Roy's."

"That's okay," I said. "He was my boss, but we weren't really friends."

Lenny handed me the cola. "Mind you, Terry's right. "I don't have many customers like Roy left. He'd come in here at six o'clock and plant himself over near the fire until throwing out time."

"What time is that?"

"Officially eleven." He grinned. "Unofficially, whenever I feel like it."

"I heard they reckon Roy was killed in a bungled burglary," Terry said.

"That's what the police reckon."

"You don't sound convinced."

"His daughter has asked me to investigate his death."

"Are you a P.I. too?"

"Yeah. Did Roy have any problems with anyone that you know of?"

The two men exchanged a glance that spoke volumes, and I thought for a moment they were about to clam up, but Lenny must have decided that I was worthy of his trust.

"There's this one guy called Ray West."

"Westy?"

"You know him?"

"Well enough for him to threaten me."

"He and Roy had a barney in here last week."

* * *

The sooner R.K. Investigations started generating cash, the better. Not only did I need to pay the rent, myself and Zero, but it would also mean I could use cabs to get around. At the moment, I was stuck with public transport. That meant a forty-minute journey on two tube trains and the DLR to get from Upney to Greenwich.

It was time to reacquaint myself with Christine's husband, Ralph. I hadn't laid eyes on him since she and I had fallen out. Until she'd mentioned it, I'd had no idea that he was working only a mile down the road from where I now lived.

I called Zero to tell him I wouldn't be back in the office because I was going to take a look at BetMore, and then I'd go straight home from there. When he asked if I'd remembered to update TimeLogMaster, I lied and said that I had. That young man was a worse nag than my mother.

BetMore was located on a side street, halfway between Greenwich and Lewford. Fortunately, there was a small tea room almost directly across the road from the betting shop, so I was able to sit down while keeping watch. The betting shop's clientele was pretty much what you'd have expected: Ninety percent male—three-quarters of whom were over fifty.

Ralph had been working in a betting shop in Purley when he and Christine had first got together. I wasn't even sure if I'd still recognise him, but I needn't have worried. My cup of tea was just starting to go cold when he stepped out of the shop. Apart from the additional pounds around his waist, and the higher hairline, he looked pretty much the same as the last time I'd seen him.

He made a left towards the high street.

I'd no way of knowing how long he'd be gone, but I decided to take my chances and have a look inside the shop. Why was it so dark in there? It's not like they couldn't afford the electricity. I'd only ever been in a betting shop once before, and that was with my dad when I was a kid. I would have been eight or nine at the time, and by rights, I shouldn't have been allowed inside, but no one seemed to care. BetMore was certainly a step up from the Leeds betting shop of my childhood. Back then, the only seats were a few old wooden stools next to the ledges where the punters wrote out their betting slips. Today's betting shop had armchairs, sofas and by the look of it, free tea and coffee.

"Hi." A young woman came out from behind the counter. "Are you okay?"

"Err — yes, thanks."

"Do you need help with anything?"

"I'm just here for the slot machines, thanks."

It didn't take a rocket scientist to work out that Susan, the assistant manager according to her badge, had to be Ralph's new love interest.

"Okay." She beamed. "Just give me a shout if you need anything. Do help yourself to a drink."

"Thanks." I shoved a pound coin in the nearest slot machine, pressed the red button, and then started for the door.

"Hold on, love!" A guy with a walking stick called after me. "You've won. You got four bells."

He was right; the coins began to clatter into the tray.

"Typical!" A young man with a cigarette stub behind his ear, scowled at me. "I've put twenty quid in that thing."

"Sorry." I collected my winnings, which according to the sticker on the front of the machine, was fifty quid for four bells.

With my trouser pockets weighed down with coins, I struggled to the door. As I stepped outside, I spotted Ralph headed back towards the shop. Fortunately, he was so engrossed in his phone that he didn't see me cross the road and walk away.

I had planned on grabbing another microwave meal on my way home, but after my unexpected windfall, I decided to treat myself to the best that the Gerbil and Oyster had to offer.

"Scampi and chips please, Kenny."

"I had a fella in here earlier asking after you."

"Who?"

"Don't know his name. Didn't get chance to ask. I told him I hadn't seen you for a day or two. He asked where you lived."

"You didn't tell him, did you?"

"Course not. I'm not stupid."

"What did he look like?"

"He had big bushy sideburns. You could definitely do

better than him. What are you drinking?"

"Give me a bottle of lager." I handed him a handful of pound coins.

"Have you been robbing the leccy meter?"

"I've just won this on a slot machine."

"Didn't know you played them. You should try ours. We've just had a new one delivered."

"It was a one-off. Where's Billy?"

"The Mrs has taken him to get his claws clipped."

Chapter 11

The scampi and chips had gone down a treat, but I didn't bother staying for a second drink because I had to call in at Suds to get my washing, which I should have collected the day before.

"Sorry I didn't make it yesterday, Elsie. Things went a bit crazy."

"No worries, Kat. It's over there on the chair."

"Thanks. I don't know what I'd do without this place."

"You might find out soon enough. The boss reckons he'll have to shut shop if they put up the business rates again."

"Are they likely to do that?"

"It wouldn't surprise me."

"What will you do if this place closes?"

"I've no idea. The launderette's all I've ever known. Fifteen years here, and eight at Washrama before that."

"Where was that?"

"In East Ham."

I hoped Suds wouldn't close. Not only for Elsie's sake, but because I didn't want to have to fork out for a washing machine. I hated the idea of having to do my own washing again. I guess my mother was right all along: I really was a lazy so and so.

As I walked past Walt's house, I noticed there was a For Sale board outside. Someone had obviously been keen to get it on the market. Out of curiosity, I fired up the property app which I'd installed on my phone the last time I moved house. When I saw the asking price, I wished I hadn't bothered; prices in this area were getting downright silly.

I was just about to go into my block of flats when Luke and Rexy came out.

"I'm sorry I couldn't take him this morning, Mrs," the boy said. "We had a school trip."

"That's okay, but do me a favour, would you?"

"What?"

"Don't call me *Mrs*. It's depressing. Call me Kat."

"That's a cool name."

"Thanks. You'd better get a move on. Rexy's doing that little shuffle he always does just before he lets rip."

The aroma in the lift confirmed my suspicion that the dog must have been clenching his buttocks on the way down. Speaking of bad smells, Leo was waiting for me outside the door to my flat.

"What do you want?" I snapped.

"That's no way to greet an old friend."

"I've had a long day. Say what you came to say, and then sling your hook."

"Do you remember I told you I was staying at my brother's gaff?"

"Sharing his squat, you mean?"

"Yeah, well we just got evicted."

"So?" I shrugged.

"Come on, Kat. You wouldn't see me sleeping on the street, would you?"

I laughed. "Did you seriously think I'd let you stay here?"

"Just for one night. Two tops."

"Let me see. How can I put this politely? Sod off and never show your face around here again or I'll be forced to punch it."

"Where am I supposed to go?"

"I neither know nor care. How about you go and see Gina? Maybe she'll take pity on you and let you stay there."

"Come on, Kat." He took a couple of steps forward, but stopped dead in his tracks when I raised my fists. "You wouldn't hit me, would you?"

"If you're not in that lift within five minutes, you'll find out."

"You always were a cow."

"Love you too, Leo."

After I'd put away the washing, I checked my phone for messages, only to find a notification on the home screen that I'd never seen before. Whatsapp? Since when did I have that installed? When I clicked on it, I was taken to chats where a message from Zero was waiting for me.

I thought you ought to have this app on your phone too. It's the easiest way for us to keep in touch. Two things: Sheila called in looking for you. She said she was just passing and wanted to let you know she'll be at the funeral. Secondly: Use the TimeLogMaster!

I tapped in a quick response.

Okay, Mum.

***

"I haven't called at a bad time, have I, Kat?"

It was my own fault. I'd told Christine she could call me any time, but I hadn't anticipated she would choose to do it just as I was about to climb into a hot bath.

"No, it's fine." I lied.

"Ralph's just texted to say he's going to be late home again."

"I called in at BetMore on my way home."

"Did you see him?"

"Yeah, but he didn't see me. I waited until he went out, and then had a quick look inside the shop."

"Did you see *her*?"

"Susan? Yeah."

"Pretty, isn't she?"

"So are you."

"I don't feel it."

"Don't be silly, Christine. This has got nothing to do with you. If Ralph's playing away, it's down to him."

"*If?* What else could he be up to? He hardly ever worked late until she started there. Couldn't you follow him?"

"Right now?"

"Yeah. He's only just texted me, so you'll probably catch them leaving if you're quick." She hesitated. "Unless you were already doing something?"

I glanced at the inviting bubbles and the bottle of red wine I'd just uncorked. "Nothing important. I'll go straight around there now."

"Thanks, Kat. You're the best."

That was me: Simply the best.

I pulled the bath plug, recorked the wine and threw on some clothes. As I sprinted down the road, I began to regret the scampi and chips, which were now sitting a little heavy. I really wasn't in shape. There had been a time when I used to run five miles every morning, but those days were a dim and distant memory now.

"Whoa!" Graham was forced to step to one side as I shot around the corner. "Are you okay, Kat?"

"Sorry, can't stop," I shouted back over my shoulder.

By the time I reached the street where BetMore was located, I was practically gasping for air. If I'd missed Ralph, I was going to be seriously cheesed off.

I was in luck. The lights in the shop were still on, and I could make out two figures inside: Ralph and Susan. I half expected them to disappear into the back together, but then the lights went out, and they both came out of the door. This might be one of the quickest cases I'd ever wrapped up. Snap a few photos of them together, pass them onto Christine, and that should be job done.

It didn't quite work out like that.

After exchanging a few words, Susan set off in the opposite direction from where I was standing. Ralph began to walk my way, so I ducked into a newsagent.

"Can I get you anything, lady?" The man behind the counter was wearing a string vest and an annoyed expression.

"I'm just browsing." I picked up the nearest magazine from the rack.

"Train spotter, are you?"

I hadn't noticed the title of the magazine until that moment: Trains and Tracks Monthly.

"Err, yeah, I'm a big fan of trains. And tracks." Just then, Ralph walked by the window. I gave it a few seconds, and then replaced the magazine in the rack. "I've already read this issue."

I daren't follow Ralph too closely because, even though it had been a while, there was still the chance that he'd recognise me. After all, I'd been the one who'd once tried to convince Christine to dump him.

As I expected, he took the tube from Greenwich.

Fortunately, the station was busy, so I was able to hide in the crowd further along the platform. The train arrived two minutes later. We took the same carriage, but I stood at the opposite end. A sweet young man offered me his seat. I wasn't sure if that was because he thought I was pregnant, old or just out of shape. I thanked him, but declined the offer because I wouldn't have been able to see my quarry if I'd been seated.

I had absolutely no idea where Ralph was headed, but my money was on either Canary Wharf or possibly Bank.

I was wrong on both counts.

After only a couple of stops, he disembarked at Mudchute on the Isle of Dogs. Staying out of sight was going to be a bigger challenge here because it was a much quieter station, so I hung back as long as I dared, and then followed at a distance. Ralph took a left out of the station and stayed on the same road for about ten minutes before taking a right. Luckily, he was so focussed on where he was headed that he never once looked behind him.

When he eventually entered one of the blocks of flats, I sprinted over to the building. An old woman was just stepping out of the only lift, so I presumed he must have taken the stairs. But to which floor?

It was time to throw caution to the wind. If he spotted me, so be it. There was no sign of him on the first floor or the second, but then, on the third floor, just as my lungs were about to collapse, I caught sight of him at the far end of the landing; someone had just opened a door and let him inside. Doing my best to look as casual as possible, I walked along the corridor and past the door, making a note of the number as I did.

Back on the DLR, I fired up Whatsapp, and sent a

message to Zero. Let's see if he could work his magic and come up with the occupier's name.

***

I'd just got off the DLR at Lewford when my phone rang; it was Christine, eager to know what I'd found out.

"He isn't with Susan."

"Are you sure? This all began when she started working there."

"I'm positive. I got to the betting shop just as they were coming out. They went in opposite directions."

"Maybe they saw you?"

"They didn't."

"Where did he go, then?"

"I'm not sure," I lied.

"What do you mean?"

"I lost him in the crowds. Sorry."

"I'll ask the little toerag when he gets home."

"You could, but if he is cheating on you, do you really think he'll tell you the truth? Just play it cool for now."

"I guess you're right."

"Call me when he says he's going to be late again. I might have more luck the next time."

"Okay. Thanks, Kat."

I deliberately hadn't told her about the flat in the Isle of Dogs because I didn't want her rushing around there. I needed to find out who it belonged to and what Ralph was up to first.

***

I'd just rerun the bath, and poured myself a glass of wine when my phone rang again. This could not be happening. If it was Christine, she'd get short shrift and no mistake.

It wasn't her.

"Mum?"

"Jen said you were going to call me. She said you promised."

"And I intended to. In fact, I was going to do it later this evening."

"You never were a good liar, Kathleen."

I'd long since given up on trying to get her to call me Kat.

"I've been really busy."

"What are you going to do now that your boss has been murdered?" So much for Jen not saying anything—the little snitch. "I've always said London isn't a safe place to live, haven't I?"

"It's really not half as bad as you imagine."

"I don't know why you can't get yourself back up here."

"I'm going to take over the agency."

"Why would you want to do that? There are plenty of jobs around here at the moment. Rosy Carter reckons they're setting on at Lidl, just down the road."

"I'd be no good in a supermarket. I wouldn't last a week."

"There are lots of eligible young men up here too. If you played your cards right, you could be married with a youngster in a few years' time."

"Sorry, Mum, there's someone at the door." I moved the phone away from my mouth, and shouted to the non-existent visitor. "I'm coming!"

"Kathleen. You should at least think about it."
"I will. Got to dash. Love you."

Chapter 12

This wasn't exactly the start to the day I'd hoped for. Although I wasn't a great believer in Best Before dates, I couldn't ignore the smell coming from the milk bottle. Nor the fact that the contents had solidified.

I'd eaten cornflakes dry before, but it wasn't fun. That left me with two options: Nip out and buy a fresh bottle of milk, or treat myself to a breakfast at Geordie's. As I still had most of my slot machine winnings, the latter option won out.

When I stepped out of the flat, young Luke was just getting into the lift with Rexy. I was about to shout and ask him to hold the doors when I remembered the flatulence factor. And anyway, a walk down the stairs would be good for me.

I'd only walked a few yards down the street when someone called my name.

"Kat! Where were you going in such a hurry yesterday?" It was Graham. Again.

"Do you always sneak up on people like that?"

"Only pretty young women."

"You do realise how creepy that sounds, right?"

"Sorry. That came out wrong. I meant—"

"I'd put that spade down before you dig yourself any deeper."

"Good idea. So, why were you in such a hurry yesterday?"

"I was working on a case."

"Chasing a bad guy?"

"Something like that. Have you lost something?"

"Sorry?"

"This is the first time I've seen you without Miles. Did you leave him in the park by mistake?"

"I woke at six and couldn't get back to sleep, so we took an earlier walk. It doesn't matter if I don't go to the park at my regular time now because the only person that I'm interested in bumping into doesn't go there anymore."

"I'll tell the Widow Manning you're missing her."

"You're a regular comedian. Where are you off to, anyway? You haven't started work already, have you?"

"I've run out of milk, so I'm going to treat myself to breakfast at Geordie's."

"Mind if I join you?"

"I can't very well stop you."

"It doesn't look like you're ever going to let me take you for a drink, so you could at least let me buy you breakfast."

"You can buy the coffee."

"Okay, deal. I've never actually been in Geordie's before. What's it like?"

"If you're on a health kick, it's probably not for you. But if you want to line your stomach with grease, then you'll love it."

"I take it the owner is from up north?"

"What do you consider to be *up north*? I assume you've never been north of Watford Gap?"

"I went to the Lake District on a hiking holiday once."

"That doesn't count. I'm from Leeds and I consider myself a northerner."

"I assume Geordie is from Newcastle?"

"There is no Geordie. The owner's name is Larry and he's from Liverpool."

"Why is the café called Geordie's, then?"

"The previous owner was a Geordie. When Larry bought it, he decided to keep the name."

After Graham had embarrassed himself by asking for an Earl Grey, and being told it was PG Tips—take it or leave it, we found a quiet table close to one of the windows that looked out onto the high street.

"Earl Grey?" I mocked.

"It never occurred to me they wouldn't have it."

"That, right there, is a sign you spend all your time in poncy, over-priced coffee shops and tea rooms."

"When did you move down here from Leeds?"

"As soon as I left school."

"Why here?"

"I wanted to get away from home. London sounded like a good idea."

"Was it?"

"With hindsight, it was a crazy thing to do. All I had were the few clothes I'd thrown into a case and the bit of money I'd saved."

"Where did you live?"

"With my Grandma Vi. She's my father's mother. I lived there until I'd found a job and could afford to pay rent on a place of my own."

"What did your parents say about you coming down here?"

"My father was already dead by then. My mother threw a fit; she hated the idea of me moving to London, but she hated the idea of me moving in with Vi even more. My mother and father split up when I was ten, and my mother has barely spoken to Vi since then."

"But you came down here anyway?"

"Yeah."

Just then, Larry brought two huge fry-ups and dropped them onto the table with his usual grace.

"I thought I'd ordered the regular?" Graham stared at the plate, which was piled high with cholesterol.

"This is the regular," I assured him. "If we'd had the large, we'd have had to eat at separate tables." I stabbed one of the sausages, and took a bite. "No one does breakfasts quite like Larry."

"How did you get into the P.I. business?"

"I just kind of fell into it. I'd worked a number of part-time jobs in cafes and bars mainly, but then I saw an ad for someone to work as a general assistant for a private investigator. A dogsbody, really. The money was rubbish, but at least it was full-time."

"Have you had any training?"

I laughed. "I'm pretty sure the Open University doesn't do P.I. courses. No, I just learned on the job. At first, I was mainly doing research, but after a while Roy got me doing bits and bobs of other stuff. It just grew from there."

"It must be interesting, though?"

"It has its moments. Anyway, enough about me. What are you doing in Lewford? You look more like a Hampstead kind of a guy."

He grinned. "What do you mean by that?"

"I'm going by the look of terror when you saw Larry put that plate in front of you. You couldn't possibly have lived around these parts all of your life without mastering the fry-up."

"You're half right. I haven't lived here long, but I certainly couldn't afford Hampstead prices."

"Where are you from originally, then?"

"Canterbury."

"Canterbury? You're not even a Londoner."

"Neither are you."

"I'm more of one than you are by the sound of it. How come you ended up living here?"

"I moved here when Sharon and I split up."

"*Sharon*?" I grinned. "Was that really her name?"

"What's wrong with Sharon?"

"There's nothing wrong with the name Sharon, but she doesn't sound like the kind of woman that you'd marry. I would have expected a Felicity or a Camilla."

"She has a job in the city, at one of the major banks."

"Doing what?"

"She's an accountant."

"A solicitor and an accountant. Sounds like a match made in hell."

"We had a flat in Limehouse until we split up."

"Where does she live now?"

"She's still there."

"With her new fella?"

"Yeah."

"And you ended up here. How come you didn't hightail it back to Canterbury?"

"I like living in London. I'm not sure I could ever go back to Canterbury now."

"So, it's just you and Miles?"

"Yes. Like I said, Rupert is allergic to dogs, so I had to take Miles."

"Rupert is the guy who's sleeping in your old bed, I take it?"

"I wouldn't have put it quite like that."

"Sharon and Rupert? I can't see that lasting very long. Maybe she'll take you back when it all goes pear-shaped."

"That's never going to happen. Sharon and I are history. What about you? What's it like being a private investigator?"

"You know that guy who sells buckets on the market on the high street?"

"Yeah?"

"Well, it's nothing like that. It's not much like being a librarian either."

"Are you ever serious?"

"Not if I can help it. Are you going to eat that last sausage?"

"I've had too much already."

"Shame to let it go to waste." I grabbed it from his plate.

"How can you eat so much and still look like you do?"

"I have a fast metabolism."

Breakfast over, we were just about to leave when I spotted Ricky Simms with his old dad, Arthur, sitting at a table at the back of the café. They must have come in while Graham and I were debating how posh he was.

"I've just spotted someone I should say hello to," I said to Graham.

"Shall I wait for you?"

"No, I might be a while."

"How about going for a drink with me tonight?"

"Sorry, no can do. I'm working undercover."

"All night?"

"Yep."

"When will you sleep?"

"When I'm dead."

"Hey, Ricky, Arthur. I didn't see you two come in."

"You were too busy whispering sweet nothings to that new fellow of yours." Arthur only had the two front teeth. One on the top and one on the bottom.

"Don't be daft, Arthur. You know I only have eyes for you."

"Don't encourage him, Kat," Ricky said.

"I haven't seen either of you for a while. Where have you been hiding?"

"I've been on the sick for a month with my back." Ricky winced as he tried to straighten it. "I did it at work."

Ricky was a dustbin man, or as they insisted on calling them today, a waste disposal technician.

"He doesn't know what hard work is," Arthur chipped in. "I used to work twelve hour shifts down the foundry."

"Eight days a week, weren't it, Arthur?"

"Don't wind him up, Kat." Ricky laughed. "You're not the one who has to live with him."

"Has he moved in with you, then?"

"Hey! I'm right here!" Arthur scolded me. "I'm not dead yet."

"Sorry, Arthur. I didn't know you'd moved in with Ricky."

"Not my idea."

"It's only temporary, Dad. I've told you that." Ricky turned to me. "He had a bit of trouble."

"Have you been poorly, Arthur?" I asked.

"No, I ain't been poorly. This one thinks I'm losing my marbles, but I can still run rings around him. And you, come to that."

"I never said you'd lost your marbles, Dad. It's just for a

couple of weeks."

"That bed of yours is too hard." Arthur stood up. "I'm going to the bookies."

"I haven't finished my breakfast yet," Ricky said.

"You can catch up with me when you have."

"Just be careful."

"Bye, Arthur," I called after him.

When he was out of the door, I asked Ricky what had been behind the decision for his father to move in with him.

"Some lowlife stole his watch and cash."

"He was mugged?"

"No, thank goodness. A guy came to the door and reckoned he was from the water company. Dad let him in, and then after he'd left, Dad realised the man had taken the watch and money. He won't admit it, but it shook him up a bit."

"How old is Arthur now?"

"Eighty-one."

"I was talking to Rose in the Gerbil the other night. Same thing happened to her old mum."

"The police never told me that."

"It might not have been the same guy, I suppose."

"What makes someone do something like that, Kat? Preying on old people? If I get hold of him, I'll kick seven shades out of him."

"You'll have to get in the queue behind Rose."

"What about your old grandmother, Kat? Does she still live on her own?"

"Vi? Yeah. Ever since I moved out."

"Has she ever thought about moving into a residential home?"

"There's only one way you'll get her out of her place, and that's feet first."

"Still, you ought to warn her about this conman. Who knows where he'll strike next?"

"Yeah, I will."

"I'd better go and find Dad before he bets away all his pension."

"See you, Ricky."

***

On my journey into the city, I was still trying to work out what I was going to do about the Premax case. When Roy had originally taken it on, the idea was that I'd work a few nightshifts instead of my normal daytime duties. Now that it was just me, I was having to work both day and night. That obviously wasn't going to work. I hated the idea of having to quit on a case, but realistically I couldn't work twenty-four hours a day. Roy had used Westy on some cases, but he and I weren't exactly on good terms at the moment. Longer term, if things worked out, I'd be able to set on another experienced P.I. with whom I could share the load, but that was a non-starter for now.

By the time I arrived at the Sidings, I'd decided that I'd have to call Kevin Lockhart, and tell him I was going to have to bow out of the Premax case.

There was a young woman in the office, sitting on Zero's desk. One look at him, told me he was smitten with her.

"Kat, this is Toyah."

"Hi, Toyah."

"Hi." She had more ear piercings than you could shake a stick at. "I hope you don't mind me dropping in to see Z."

"Not at all. He was just about to make me a cup of coffee, weren't you, Zero?"

"Looks like it."

"Would you like one, Toyah?" I offered.

"No, thanks. I've got to get to work." She leaned over and gave him a kiss. "See ya."

Zero brought my coffee through a few minutes later.

"I take it that you and Toyah are an item?"

"Yeah. For two years now."

"I noticed she called you Z. Do you prefer that?"

"I don't mind much either way. I call her T most of the time."

"T and Z? That's sweet."

"Shut up." He blushed.

"What does Toyah do?"

"She works in a sushi bar."

"Around here?"

"No. Near Tottenham Court Road. She's actually a qualified aromatherapist, but there are no job openings in that field at the moment."

"Right."

"Kat, you've not been logging your time properly."

"Guilty as charged. I am getting better at it, though. Anyway, you may as well remove one of the cases from the system. When I've finished this coffee, I'm going to give Kevin Lockhart at Premax a call to tell him they'll have to find someone else to take over the case."

"Why would you do that?"

"I can't work all day and all night too. Something has to give, and Premax is the obvious candidate."

"But I haven't finished checking their CCTV yet."

"You managed to access it, then?"

"Of course I did. Piece of cake. I've run through it a couple of times, but so far there's nothing much to see." He grinned. "Except for you in those awful overalls."

"They were standard issue."

"I would hope so. I'd hate to think you'd worn them voluntarily. I was planning to give the footage a closer look just in case I missed something."

"Don't waste any more time on it. We're done with that case."

***

Kevin Lockhart was quite understanding when I explained that I was going to have to drop his case. If it hadn't been for Roy's death, I'm pretty sure he would have given me a much harder time, and I wouldn't have blamed him because we'd well and truly dropped the ball this time.

Zero popped his head around my door. "Got a minute?"

"Yeah, come in."

"How did the guy at Premax take it?"

"He was quite reasonable under the circumstances. I'm not sure I'd have been so understanding in his position."

"Do you want me to bill him for the time you've already spent on the case?"

"I didn't discuss that with him."

"He was paying by the hour, wasn't he? Not on results."

"True, but it just doesn't feel right."

"Insolvency will feel a whole lot worse. Why don't I just bill him and see what happens?"

"Yeah, okay. Nothing to lose, I guess."

"By the way, I found out who's living in that flat in the Isle of Dogs."

"Who is it?"

"As far as I can make out, there's just the one occupant: a woman named Deborah Todman."

"That sounds promising."

"Maybe not. She's fifty-nine years old."

"That would make her almost thirty years older than Ralph. Somehow, I can't see her being the other woman. Are you sure there isn't anyone else living there?"

"I can't be one-hundred percent positive, but she's the only one showing on all the records: council, utilities, electoral roll. Maybe she's a relative of his?"

"If that was the case, why wouldn't he just tell Christine where he was going? I reckon there must be someone else staying there. Ideally, I'd stake out the flat to see who comes and goes, but there's no chance of that. I need to focus on finding Roy's murderer, and the Fulton case."

"I could do it. I could stake out the flat."

"Don't be stupid."

"Why is it stupid?"

"I brought you in to work here in the office."

"Your case management system is up to date, your social media is all sorted, and I can't set up the accounts until you get those books."

"I looked for them at Roy's house, but no joy. Maybe

they're in his car. I'll have to ask his daughter what happened to them."

"So, why don't I watch the flat?"

"I need someone here to answer the phones."

"You sound like my grandma."

"Hey, watch it."

"I can divert all the calls to my mobile. What's the point in me sitting here with nothing to do?"

"You don't have any experience of surveillance."

"How difficult can it be to watch a flat? And let's be honest, no one would suspect me of being there on surveillance, would they?"

"That's true. They'd be more likely to think you were casing the joint."

"Thanks."

"No offence."

"Does that mean I can do it?"

"I suppose so.

"When do I start?"

"No time like the present."

"Great."

"I want a photo of everyone who goes in or out of that flat."

"Sweet. If Deborah Todman leaves, shall I follow her?"

"No. She's not the one we're interested in. I want to know who else lives there, or visits there."

"Okay."

"One other thing." I handed him a slip of paper with Lisa's phone number on it. "Can you keep trying this number? It belongs to a woman named Lisa. I've tried it a dozen times already, but she isn't picking up. If she does answer, tell her I'd like to speak to her as a matter of urgency about Mike Dale. She can call me on my mobile, or if she'd prefer, I can meet her somewhere."

"Will do."

"If you do manage to contact her, text me, will you?"

"I'll Whatsapp you."

"Whatever. Just let me know. And Zero, don't make me regret this."

Chapter 13

My phone rang.

"Kat, can you hear me?"

"I can hear you, Vi."

"I didn't think this phone was working."

"It seems to be okay."

"That's strange because I couldn't think of any other reason you wouldn't have called me for two weeks."

Vi had mastered the art of the *burn* long before the term had even been coined.

"I'm sorry, but things have been really crazy recently."

"What are you doing tonight?"

"I—err." I had expected to be working the nightshift at Premax, but now my evening was free. "Nothing much, actually."

"Why don't you pop over for dinner? It's your favourite: corned beef hash."

As a Londoner all her life, I was prepared to forgive Vi for incorrectly referring to tea as dinner. "That sounds great. What time shall I come over?"

"Mrs Grove has asked me to look after her Rhubarb this afternoon, so you'd better make it six."

It was just as well that I knew Rhubarb was her neighbour's Chihuahua. "What will Catzilla make of that?"

"I wish you wouldn't call Lulu that horrible name."

"Sorry."

"I have to keep them in separate rooms."

I wasn't in the least surprised. Lulu, AKA Catzilla, was a nightmare of a cat. Given half a chance, she would have chewed up the little dog and spit him out.

"Okay. I'll see you later."

***

I had expected there to be CCTV at Fulton Associates, but a quick call to Ted Fulton had established that there were no cameras inside or outside their offices. All was not yet lost, though. Maybe there would be cameras on the nearby buildings.

The buildings either side of Fulton Associates were unoccupied, but across the road, I struck gold. The bar, Top Heavy, brought a whole new meaning to the word sleazy. It had a neon sign in the window that read: Exotic Dancers – Seven Nights A Week.

I could see very little through the tinted windows, so I took a deep breath and ventured inside. It transpired that there was nothing much to see on the ground floor except for more posters advertising the exotic dancers and happy hour. The bar itself was in the basement.

Downstairs, the lighting was low, and the carpets sticky. With what, I didn't care to imagine. The place was practically deserted.

"Have you come about the job, love?" The man behind the bar had a toupee balanced precariously on his head. "Did you bring your costume?"

"What does she need a costume for?" The drunk, who was propped up on a stool next to the bar, undressed me with his bloodshot eyes.

"I'm not here about a job."

"You sure? We pay top dollar to our girls. You would work three shows, five days a week, and all the tips you can make. A looker like you would do well."

"No, thanks. I wanted to ask someone about your CCTV."

"You a cop? There are no drugs in here. I won't stand for them."

"I'm not a cop."

"All our girls are old enough. I make them bring in their birth certificates."

"I'm just interested in the CCTV."

"Why?"

"I'm a private investigator."

"Bit of a sleazy job for a woman that, isn't it?"

"I've been hired to find a man who has gone missing. He worked in the offices directly across the road. I was hoping I might be able to check your CCTV footage for the day he disappeared. It's just possible it may have caught him on there."

"No skin off my nose. Do you know how to work it?"

"Yeah," I lied.

"Come on, then. I'll show you where it is."

It turned out that Brad, that was the manager's name, wasn't the total lowlife I'd had him down as. Not only did he set me up in his office with the CCTV, he even brought me a cup of coffee, on the house. It tasted like rat pee, but it's the thought that counts.

I could have done with Zero there to help me because I wasn't the least bit techie. After a couple of false starts, I eventually got to grips with the controls. Luckily, it seemed that Brad never wiped the recordings, which seemed to go back several months. I knew the date that Mike Dale had gone missing, and that he'd worked a full day at the office on that particular day, so I started to view the tape from four-thirty onwards.

The footage wasn't great because it was focussed on the pavement on this side of the road. However, the offices of Fulton Associates were visible in the background, and I was able to zoom in on the main doors to watch the comings and goings. At six-thirty-five, according to the timestamp, Mike Dale came out of one of the automatic doors, and turned left.

In his hand, he was carrying a laptop computer.

"Did you find what you wanted, love?" Brad shouted when I returned to the bar.

"Yes, I think so. Thanks for your help."

"No worries. If you ever decide you'd like to make a bit of extra cash in the evenings, there's a job here for you."

"Thanks, I'll bear that in mind."

Mike Dale's PA had told me that her boss never took his laptop home with him, so why had he taken it that day? Had he known that he wouldn't be returning? And why had Ted Fulton told Tas that the computer was in for repair? I really did need to speak to Lisa, but there were no messages from Zero which suggested he hadn't been able to get hold of her either.

***

The business with Westy was still weighing heavily on my mind. I hadn't yet ruled him out as Roy's murderer, but it was also possible that it could have been someone related to one of the cases that he'd been working on. I wasn't particularly worried about his veiled threats because he would have had to be a complete idiot to attack me so soon after Roy's murder. To do so would have been to shine a spotlight on himself.

It was time to give him a call.

"It's Kat."

"Have you got my money?"

"That's what I want to talk to you about."

"What is there to talk about? I just want my money."

"Can we meet?"

"Only if you're going to bring the cash."

"Okay. Where?"

"I'll come to your office."

"That doesn't work for me. I want to meet somewhere there'll be lots of people around."

"Don't you trust me, Kat?"

"No."

"Sensible girl." He laughed. "Do you know Rita's Café? It's in Bloomsbury."

"I'll find it. What time?"

"Two o'clock. Don't be late because I'm not going to hang around waiting for you."

***

I caught the tube to Russell Square, and soon found the café. I was twenty minutes early.

Still feeling flush from my slot machine win, I treated myself to a millionaire's shortbread with my coffee.

Thirty minutes later, there was no sign of Westy. What little coffee I had left was now cold, but there were no free top-ups, and I wasn't paying for another cup of that slop. I tried Westy's number, but there was no answer. Maybe he'd been delayed on the tube.

Another three quarters of an hour later, and the café owner was glaring at me. I couldn't blame her; it was only a small café and I'd been sitting there with an empty cup for the best part of an hour. I'd tried to call Westy a dozen times, but with no success. The TFL website didn't show any delays on the tube, so it couldn't have been down to that. I doubted he'd simply stood me up because he wanted that money.

Whatever the reason, it was obvious he was a no-show, so I took my empty cup to the counter—it was the least I could do under the circumstances.

On my way back to the tube station, I gave my new assistant a call.

"How's it going, Zero?"

"I'm cold."

"You were the one who wanted to work surveillance. Have you seen anyone?"

"Just the one woman. She's really old—at least fifty."

"Ancient, then. I assume that's Deborah Todman. Did you get a photo?"

"Yeah. Shall I send it to you?"

"Yes, please."

Seconds later, my phone beeped with a Whatsapp message. The woman certainly looked the right age to be Todman.

"She didn't clock you, did she?"

"Of course not. Mind you, I'm not sure she'd have noticed me even if I'd been juggling, stark naked. She looked miles away. A bit of a miserable cow too if you ask me."

"What was she doing?"

"She nipped out to the shops. She must have gone somewhere local because she was back in twenty minutes."

"Is that all?"

"So far, yes. What time do you want me to stay here until?"

"You can call it a day at seven, but I'm going to need you there again first thing in the morning?"

"Six o'clock?"

"I was going to say seven, but six would be even better."

"Okay."

I had to hand it to the lad, he was keen.

***

My Grandma Vi lived just up the road from me in New Cross, which made the fact that I hadn't seen her in over a fortnight all the worse.

"It's me, Vi."

"I'm in the kitchen, Kat. Would you like a cuppa? Dinner will be ready for six-thirty."

"Yes, please."

Her kitchen was almost as big as my entire flat. She and my late grandfather had moved into the terraced house in the sixties, long before property prices had started to go insane.

"Can I help with anything?"

"No. Grab a seat and tell me your news."

"There's nothing much to report. Just the same old same old."

"Don't give me that old tosh. I might be getting on a bit, but I'm not stupid. I saw that boss of yours went and got himself murdered. I was just keeping my fingers crossed that you weren't the one who did it."

"You can rest easy. It wasn't me."

"Who did it, then?"

"I don't know. The police reckon it was a burglary gone wrong, but I don't buy that."

"The Old Bill never did have a clue. Look what happened with my washing line."

Not long after I'd moved in with Vi, someone had helped themselves to my underwear from the clothesline. I'd told Vi it would be a waste of time calling the police, but she'd insisted. They'd sent around a male uniformed officer who'd taken a few notes and made a few inappropriate wisecracks. We'd neither seen nor heard from him again. Fortunately, the incident had been a one-off.

"I've taken over the P.I. agency, Vi."

"Good for you, girl. You can't make a worse job of it than that loser who employed you. What does your mother have to say about it?"

"She's not very thrilled. She reckons I should move back home and get a job in Lidl."

"I'm surprised you told her about the murder."

"I wouldn't have done, but I made the mistake of mentioning it to Jen, the day after she came down here. I asked her not to say anything to Mum, but—"

"Jen came down?"

Me and my big mouth. "Err—yeah, last weekend."

"Why didn't you bring her to see me?"

Normally, I would have covered for Jen, but seeing as

how she'd thrown me under the bus with my mother, I didn't see why I should. "I tried to, but she was scared of what Mum might say."

"It isn't fair of your mother to stop my only other grandchild from visiting me."

"You must know by now that Mum's never going to change."

"At least I have you." She planted a kiss on top of my head.

Just then, Catzilla made her entrance, and gave me that look of hers.

"The cat's here." I shuffled my legs under the table.

"I don't know why you're so scared of Lulu. She's a little darling. Why don't you pick her up and give her a stroke?"

Because, judging by the way the cat was looking at me, she would have ripped my throat out if I'd even tried.

"I think she's hungry."

"Her food is in the cupboard by the door. Put her some out, would you, Kat?"

I walked gingerly across the kitchen, never once taking my eyes off Catzilla. I was convinced if I'd looked away, she would have launched an attack.

The cat food smelled awful, but Catzilla made short work of it, and then, much to my relief, she made her way out.

The corned beef hash hit the spot as it always did.

"Let me do the washing up, Vi."

"Don't be stupid. I've got a dishwasher to do that." She walked over to the sideboard, took an envelope out of the drawer, and stuffed it into my hand.

"What's this?"

"Just a bit of cash to keep you going."

"I can't take your money, Vi."

"You'll take it or get a slap. It can't be easy for you now your boss has gone and got himself murdered. It isn't much, but it'll help you until you get on your feet."

"I'll pay you back."

"No, you won't. What do I want money for? I've got everything I need. Except for a toy boy. You don't know where I could find myself one of those, do you?"

"I'll keep my eyes peeled for you."

"What about you? Are you seeing anyone?"

"Not at the moment. Leo came sniffing around yesterday."

"I hope you told him where to go."

"Don't worry. I've got enough on my plate without dating a married man. There is this one guy that I've seen a few times in the park when I've taken the dog for a walk."

"I didn't know you had a dog."

"I have a part share in one."

"How did you manage that?"

I told her all about Walt and how I'd agreed to share the dog with the Widow Manning.

"What kind of person calls a dog The Brick?"

"Walt was a bit of a one-off. We're calling the dog Rexy now, anyway."

"The guy in the park? He isn't married, is he?"

"No. He was engaged, but his fiancée dumped him. He's from Canterbury."

"Posh then?"

"A bit. I thought he was going to have a seizure when

he saw the size of a Geordie's fry-up."

"When are you going to move in with him, then?"

"I'm not. I barely know him."

"Don't wait too long. Take it from me, life's very short."

"I'll bear that in mind. You don't keep a lot of cash in the house, do you?"

"Mind your own beeswax."

"It's just that there's been a conman going around, talking his way into people's houses."

"Why are you telling me? Do you think I'm stupid enough to let some stranger in the house?"

"No, of course not. I just thought I'd mention it."

"I might be old, but I've not lost my marbles yet."

"Sorry. Do you know Rose from the fruit stall on the market?"

"Everyone does."

"Her old mum had her jewellery nicked."

"Phoebe? I'm not surprised. She never had any sense, not even when she was young."

"Arthur Ballard too."

"Arthur? That's awful. They should string up whoever's doing this."

"So, you'll be careful, then?"

"You don't have to worry about me, Kat."

***

I bumped into Patricia Cullum who lived a few doors down from Vi. Her mother, Sarah, and Vi had been great friends for years until Sarah had passed away a couple of years before.

"Hey, Kat." Pat took a suck on one of those electronic

ciggies. "I haven't seen you for a while."

"I've been busy. How long have you been vaping?"

"It's Johnny's idea. It's supposed to wean me off the real thing."

"How's that working out?"

"I've cut down to twenty a day."

"From how many?"

"I was getting through double that."

"Good for you."

"You've been to see Vi, I assume?"

"Yeah. She gave me a bit of a hard time because I hadn't been around for a while."

"She's a tough old bird."

"You're not wrong. I still worry about her, though. Living here all by herself."

"You'll never get her out of that house."

"I know. You'd call me if there was ever a problem, wouldn't you?"

"Course I would. I've still got your number on my phone."

"Thanks, Pat."

There were five-hundred pounds in the envelope. I didn't feel too bad about taking the money because I knew Vi had a few bob, but you'd never have known it to look at her. The money would certainly help until I saw some cash coming in from the cases I was working on. And better still, the taxman couldn't get his hands on any of it.

I walked it home because even I wasn't lazy enough to take a bus from there. When I reached the high street, I bumped into Graham and Miles.

"I thought you said that you were working tonight?"

"There was a last minute change of plan."

"Hmm?"

"It's true. I was supposed to be working undercover all night, but I've had to drop the case."

"Is that the truth or is it just your way of giving me the brush-off?"

"If I wanted to give you the brush-off, don't you think I'd just do it? I wouldn't make up silly stories."

"In that case, can we get a drink later tonight?"

"Not tonight. I'm beat."

"Tomorrow night, then?"

"Okay. You've worn me down."

"Great. Where would you like to go? Anywhere. Just name it."

"The Gerbil."

"What? Seriously? It's a dump."

"I wouldn't let Kenny hear you say that. He'll set Billy on you."

"Who's Billy? The doorman?"

"He's the parrot."

"Okay, the Gerbil it is. What time?"

"It depends what happens tomorrow. I don't work nine-to-five like you, City Boy."

"How about I give you my number. You can call me. Or text."

"Sounds like a plan."

Chapter 14

The next morning, I was just about to set off for the office when there was a knock at the door. If that was Leo, he'd be headed back down to the ground floor without the aid of either the stairs or lift.

It was Luke.

"Good morning, young man. Rexy's at the Widow Manning's."

"I know that, Mrs."

"What did I tell you about calling me that?"

"Sorry, Kat."

"Are you here to say you can't walk him this morning?"

"No. My dad said I had to tell you what happened last night."

"What did happen?"

"I was in the park with Rexy when a bloke came up to me. He wanted to know where you lived."

"Who was he? Do you know him?"

"No, but he reckoned that Rexy bit his kid."

"Right. Did the man have his lying little toerag of a son with him?"

"No, he was by himself. I told him that Rexy would never bite anyone."

"What did he say to that?"

"That I should keep my nose out and my mouth shut."

"Did he threaten you?"

"Not really. He doesn't scare me."

"You should have given him my address. I don't want you taking risks on my behalf."

"I did give him an address." Luke grinned. "It wasn't yours, though."

"Whose was it?"

"Nobody's, probably. I just made it up."

"Stay there. I'll get my shoes on, and I'll come with you to the park this morning."

"There's no need. I'm not scared."

"Humour me. It will make me feel better."

We collected the dog from the Widow Manning, and then made our way downstairs. Luke and Rexy took the lift; I took the stairs. I was no fool.

Graham was in the park with Miles.

"Hey, Kat. I wasn't expecting to see you until tonight."

"Do you remember those kids who were taunting Rexy?"

"They haven't been at it again, have they?"

"No, but the lad, whose coat Rexy bit, sent his father after me. He collared Luke last night to try and find out where I lived."

"Did he pay you a visit?"

"No. The youngster gave him a made-up address."

"Good for Luke."

"I thought I should come with him this morning in case the guy came back."

"If you need any help, let me know."

"It's okay, City Boy, I can handle it."

"Is that your official nickname for me? City Boy?"

"Until I come up with a better one, yeah."

"Do I get to call you by a nickname?"

"No."

"That seems fair."

The little toerag's dad was a no-show.

"I'm not sure you should take Rexy out by yourself, Luke," I said. "Not until I've had a word with this man."

"I'll be alright, Mrs, I mean Kat. Honest."

"Do you have a phone?"

"Of course I do."

It was a stupid question. Which kid didn't have one these days?

"Give it here. I'll add my number to your contacts. If you see the man again, call or text me straight away. Got it?"

"Yep."

"And if he asks you for my address, give him the real one this time. Okay?"

"Yep."

"Are we still on for tonight?" Graham called to me as I was on my way out of the park.

"Yeah, work permitting."

"Are you sure you don't want to change your mind about the Gerbil? I can think of a million better places to go. To be honest, I can't think of anywhere worse."

"The Gerbil will be fine. I'll call you."

***

I bumped into Sonya on my way to the Sidings.

"Hey, Kat, do you want to join me for breakfast?"

"I probably shouldn't. I'm supposed to be on a get fit regime."

"Stuff that for a game of soldiers." She laughed. "Come on. Just think of all that lovely fried bread dipped in a runny egg."

My resistance crumbled, and I joined her in Joe's, where we both had the full English.

"It doesn't get better than this." She shovelled a forkful of baked beans into her mouth. "Did you get your business cards sorted out?"

"Yeah. I went to see Vic like you said. By the way, do you know what happened to his ear?"

"Not really. I did ask him once, and he said a monkey bit it off in the jungle, but I reckon he was joking."

"I hope so. Oh, by the way, Sheila has resigned."

"When?"

"Earlier this week. I've taken on a young lad."

"Why didn't you give me a call?"

"I thought about it, but I needed someone full-time, and I can't be sure the business will even be here in a month. I didn't think you'd want to take that risk."

"Fair enough. What's he like?"

"A bit weird, but so far, I'm impressed. His name is Zero. You might have seen him knocking around the Sidings. His hair sticks out at a weird angle; I've never seen anything quite like it."

"I think I know who you mean. He popped into our place to hand in his CV." She grinned. "Mind you, he soon ran away when he saw some of our stock. I think it blew his young mind. What did you say his name was again?"

"Zero."

"He must have made that up."

"He reckons not. Zero Smith, apparently."

"Poor kid. I bet his school days were fun. I tell you what, it's been ages since you and I had a night out. How about we get blotto tonight?"

"I can't. I — err — I've already got something planned."

"Oh yeah? What's his name?"

"What makes you think it's a guy?"

"I can sense these things. Who is he?"

"No one. Just someone I bump into occasionally when I take the dog in the park."

"What's he like?"

"Posh, at least according to my Grandma Vi."

"Has she met him?"

"No, but he comes from Canterbury. That's enough for her to pass judgement."

"So, come on, spill the beans. What's his name?"

"Graham."

"What does he do for a living?"

"What's with the Spanish Inquisition?"

"I like to keep abreast of these things. If things work out between you two, don't forget I can get you a discount off any of our stock."

"Jeez, Sonya. I haven't even had a drink with the guy yet."

***

When I arrived at the Sidings, there was a police car in the car park. Who were they delivering bad news to this time?

"Good morning, Kat." DCI Menzies was waiting for me outside my offices; Constable Sharp was with him. "Can we go inside, please?"

"What's this all about?"

"It would be better if we spoke inside."

I unlocked the door, and led them through to my office.

"I heard on the grapevine that you intend to keep this place going." Menzies smirked. He seemed to do that a lot in my company.

"That's the plan. What's this all about?"

"Do you know a man called Ray West?"

"Westy? Yeah, he used to do some work for Roy."

"When was the last time you saw him?"

"He came into the office earlier this week. Tuesday, I think."

"What did he want?"

"He reckoned Roy owed him money for work that he'd done, and he expected me to pay him."

"Did you?"

"No. I told him to sling his hook."

"Ray West is known to be a violent man. I can't imagine he reacted well to being told he wasn't getting his money."

"Is that a question?"

"Yes. How did he react when you said you weren't going to pay him?"

"He wasn't best pleased."

"Did he threaten you?"

"He might have. I wasn't really paying attention."

"And you haven't seen him since then?"

"No."

"Are you sure?"

"I was supposed to meet him yesterday afternoon at Rita's Café in Bloomsbury, but he didn't show up."

"Why were you going to meet him?"

"I'd told him that I was going to give him his money. That's the only way I could get him to agree to see me. It was a lie, though. I just wanted to talk to him about the cases he'd been working on for Roy. Do you want to tell me what this is all about?"

"Ray West was murdered yesterday afternoon."

"What? Where?"

"We can discuss that back at the station."

"Are you arresting me?"

"Of course not. We'd just like you to answer a few questions."

"And if I refuse?"

"I wouldn't advise that."

***

Although, technically, I could probably have refused their request to go down to the police station, to do so would no doubt have come back to haunt me eventually. It's not like I had anything to hide, and I figured I might even learn something to my advantage.

After a couple of hours of going over and over the same ground, I was beginning to regret my decision to cooperate.

"Tell me again why you were going to meet West yesterday." Even Menzies was starting to sound bored by his own questions.

"As I've said three times already, I wanted to find out what cases he'd been working on for Roy."

"Surely your ex-boss would have kept his own records?"

"You'd have thought so, wouldn't you? But there's no sign of them in the office or in Roy's house."

"You've been in Roy King's house since he was murdered?"

"I've already told you that. Why are you asking me the same questions over and over again?"

"Humour me, please. I want to make sure we have your *story* correct."

"Roy's daughter gave me permission to look around his house. I was trying to find the books."

"And did you?"

"For the millionth time, no. They weren't there."

"Where do you think they are?"

"I don't know. Maybe in his car."

"There was nothing like that in Mr King's car. We searched it from top to bottom."

"I have no idea, then. Maybe Westy had taken them. Have you searched his house?"

"As far as we can ascertain, Mr West doesn't appear to have had a permanent residence."

"Where did he live, then?"

"We're still trying to establish that. Do you know?"

"I've no idea. He always used to drop by the office to collect his money."

"And you asked him to meet you in Bloomsbury because you owed him money?"

"Don't put words into my mouth. What I said was that Westy reckoned Roy owed him money, and he thought because I'd taken over the business, the debt should pass to me."

"But you didn't agree?"

"Of course I didn't. He wouldn't even tell me what the payment was supposed to be for."

"His death is rather convenient for you, isn't it? It wipes out your debt."

"Are you suggesting I knocked off Westy to save myself

a grand?"

"People have killed for less."

"This is a joke." I stood up. "Unless you have any new questions for me, I'm leaving."

"You haven't asked how Mr West was killed."

"I assumed you wouldn't tell me."

"Or you already know." He walked over to the door. "Okay, you can leave, but we may need to speak to you again."

His unfounded insinuation that I knew something about Westy's murder wasn't lost on me, but I decided to let it go. I just wanted to get out of that place.

***

There was no offer of a lift back to the office, but then I would probably have refused it anyway. While being questioned, I'd had my phone on silent. A quick check showed I had several missed calls from Zero. There was a WhatsApp message from him too. It read simply:

Where are you, Kat? Call me.

Something was clearly amiss.

"Zero, it's me."

"Where have you been?"

"Never mind that. What's wrong?"

"The woman in the flat has been taken away in an ambulance."

"When?"

"About an hour ago."

"Are you sure?"

"Yeah. Well, I think so."

"What do you mean *you think so*? Weren't you

watching?"

"I'd just nipped down the road for a sandwich."

"You did *what?*"

"I hadn't had anything to eat all day. I was starving."

"You should have taken something with you. When you're on surveillance, you never take your eyes off the target. Tell me what happened."

"I was only gone for a few minutes. Ten tops. When I got back there was an ambulance parked in front of the block of flats. I didn't really think much of it, but when I got upstairs, a paramedic was coming out of the woman's flat."

"But you didn't actually see them take her to the ambulance?"

"No, but I did ask the paramedic if the person they'd taken to the ambulance was the woman from the flat. He said it was."

"Did you ask which hospital they were taking her to?"

"No, sorry. I didn't think to do that."

"Okay. Never mind. You may as well go back to the office, and I'll meet you there."

***

I'd been back at the office for half an hour before Zero showed up.

"I screwed up, Kat. I'm sorry. I shouldn't have gone for a sandwich."

"No, you shouldn't, but you're new to the job, and it's not like you've had any training. You'll know better next time, right?"

His face lit up. "You're going to let me do it again?"

"I don't see why not. You've seen how things are around here; I need all the help I can get. There are a couple of conditions, though."

"Okay?"

"First, you still have to be able to cover calls to this office."

"That's easy enough. There aren't any."

"Hopefully, that won't always be the case."

"What's the other condition?"

"That you take a snack with you, and you develop a strong bladder."

"I can do that. Where were you when I tried to call?"

"You'd better sit down, and I'll bring you up to speed."

I spent the next few minutes telling him about Westy's murder and my interrogation at the police station.

"I've never known anyone who was murdered before," he said.

"You didn't exactly know Westy."

"No, but I spoke to him just a few days ago. It's just as well my mum doesn't know what I'm doing here. She'd have a fit."

"What does she think you're doing?"

"I just told her I was working in an office."

"You should have told her you worked at BuyVrator."

He blushed. "Have you seen inside that place?"

"Yeah. Sonya, a friend of mine, works there. She often pops down here for a chat. She mentioned that you'd dropped in there to hand in your CV. She also said she'd never seen anyone leave so quickly."

"Can we get back to talking about Westy?"

"Sorry, I didn't mean to embarrass you," I lied. "I guess

my original theory is well and truly blown out of the water."

"Which was?"

"I had Westy down as the main suspect for Roy's murder. I figured he'd lost patience because Roy hadn't paid him."

"It's back to square one, then?"

"Not necessarily. The police seem to be treating the two murders separately, but what if the same person is responsible for both?"

"Is that likely?"

"It's more likely than a burglary gone wrong. What if the murderer is connected to one of the cases that Westy was working on for Roy? Maybe one of them upset the wrong person."

"But according to the paperwork that I saw, Westy wasn't working on any cases when he was killed."

"He must have been. Why else would he have been demanding payment?"

"How can you find out what he was working on?"

"If we could find the books, that might give us a clue. The only other possibility is if Westy had some paperwork that we haven't seen."

"I don't suppose you'll be able to check his place. The police will have it sealed off, won't they?"

"It's worse than that. According to the police, he doesn't appear to have had a place."

Chapter 15

Zero had made me a cup of tea. At least, I think that's what it was.

"How do you mean, Westy didn't have a place?" he said. "Was he homeless?"

"I doubt it. More likely, he was living off the grid. If I was guessing, I'd say that our Mr West didn't pay any taxes. As far as I can gather, Roy always used to pay him in cash."

"He must have been living somewhere?"

"Yeah, but the chances of our finding out where that was are pretty slim. Wherever it was, I'll wager he was using a false name and paying in cash. Somewhere where no questions are asked. He probably moved around a lot too."

"What do we do now?"

"We have to find those accounts. It's the only chance we have of finding out what Westy was working on. The only other sniff of a lead I have is the guy with bushy sideburns."

"You haven't mentioned him before."

"He was hanging around Roy's house. The next-door neighbour said he did a runner when she tried to talk to him. He also turned up at my local pub, asking for me."

"And you have no idea who he is?"

"None. It's Roy's funeral on Tuesday. Maybe he'll show up there."

"What do you want me to do about that flat in the Isle of Dogs?"

"There isn't much else you can do. There's no point in staking out the place if no one is living there. I'll just have to wait until Ralph tells Christine he's working late again, and see where he goes then."

"I could follow him if you like. You did say that he might recognise you."

"Maybe, but for now I'm more concerned about the Mike Dale case."

"Did you have any joy with the CCTV?"

"The bar across the road has cameras facing Fulton's offices. It caught Mike Dale leaving on the Friday night that he disappeared; he had his laptop with him."

"Is that significant?"

"I think so, for two reasons: First, Ted Fulton lied about the laptop. He told Dale's PA that it had been taken in for repair. And, according to his PA, Mike Dale never took his laptop home with him. So why did he take it that day?"

"Because there was something on it that he didn't want anyone else to see?"

"Perhaps. Or maybe he knew he wouldn't be coming back."

"Do you think he disappeared on purpose?"

"It's a definite possibility, but I really need to speak to Lisa. I take it you didn't have any joy getting hold of her?"

"No. I tried at least twenty times."

"That's beginning to look like another dead end."

"Not necessarily."

"What do you mean?"

"We can't make her pick up her phone, but it's definitely still switched on."

"So?"

"So, I could probably trace it."

"How?"

"It's probably best that you don't know. It's not exactly

legal."

"Jeez, Zero. When you said you used to be a hacker, I thought you were just messing with me. You really are into this stuff, aren't you?"

"I used to be, big time, but I packed in the heavy stuff when they started to get too close for comfort."

"*They*?"

"The government, secret service, that kind of thing."

"This just gets worse and worse."

"It's okay as long as you don't end up getting extradited. There are some places where they don't mess around. They'll lock you up and throw away the key for this kind of stuff."

"But you've stopped doing it now, right?"

"The serious stuff, yeah. My mum said she'd kill me if I got sent down."

"I don't want you to try to trace Lisa's phone if it's going to get you locked up."

"This kind of stuff is nothing. There are ten-year old kids who do this sort of thing in their lunchbreak at school."

"That's a scary thought. Do you really think you might be able to track down Lisa?"

"Yeah, provided she doesn't ditch her phone. I'll do it this weekend. I ought to have something for you by Monday."

"Great. We might as well call it a day. There's not much more we can do here now."

"Err, Kat — I — err — ?"

"Yeah? Spit it out."

"I was just wondering when I might get paid?"

"You've only been working here for a couple of days."

"I know. I was hoping I could get paid weekly? I'm not sure I'll last a month without any cash."

"I can try, but it isn't going to be easy until I start to see some money coming in."

"Hello!" A woman's voice came from the outer office. "Is there anyone home?"

"We're through here," I shouted.

It was Mrs Marston. "I'm sorry to interrupt."

"That's okay. This is my new assistant, Zero."

"Hi." He nodded.

"Nice to meet you, err —"

"Zero."

"Right. I just popped over to bring you this, Kat." She opened her handbag, took out a cheque and handed it to me. "And I wanted to thank you for being so honest. I'm sure a lot of people would have milked it for as much as they could get."

"No problem. I hope things work out okay for you."

"So do I, but if they don't, I know where to find you. Okay, thanks again. Bye."

I waited until I'd heard her close the outer door before taking out the envelope that Vi had given me. "Looks like you're in luck, Zero." I counted out a hundred pounds and handed it to him. "We'll sort out a proper wage for you next week. Will that keep you going until then?"

"Yeah, that's great. Thanks, Kat. See you on Monday."

***

Before my 'date' with Graham, I planned on accompanying Luke to the park, just in case the toerag's father turned up again.

"There was a man here, looking for you, Kat." The Widow Manning handed me Rexy's lead.

"Was it the guy who reckons the dog bit his lad?"

"I don't think so. At least, he didn't mention the dog."

"What did he want?"

"He didn't say. He just asked if I knew when you'd be back."

"What did he look like?"

"Tall, fiftyish, with—err—" She ran a finger down each side of her face.

"Sideburns?"

"Yeah. Bushy ones."

"How long ago was this?"

"A couple of hours, I'd say."

Just then, the lift doors pinged open; it was Luke.

"I'm going to come with you to the park," I said.

"What for?" He pouted. "I told you I'm not afraid of that bloke."

"I know you aren't, but it's time he and I had a little chat." I handed him the lead. "It's okay, I won't cramp your style if your girlfriend is there."

"I don't have a girlfriend," he said, indignantly. "Girls are stupid."

"Gee, thanks."

"You're not a girl. You're old."

"Even better. Come on, let's get going."

This time, I went with them in the lift, but not before I'd taken a huge breath, which I managed to hold until we got out on the ground floor.

Once in the park, Luke let the dog off the lead, and was soon on poop-scooping duty. His business finished, Rexy made for his favourite spot behind the bushes at the far side of the park. Luke followed him, but I stayed put, close to the gates.

Twenty minutes later, I was just about to call Luke, to tell him it was time we went back, when—

"Hey, you! I want a word!" The man was standing next to the little toerag who had attacked Rexy. They looked like two extremely ugly Russian dolls.

"Are you talking to me?"

"Your dog bit my lad, and I want to know what you're going to do about it."

"And your name is?"

"Charlie Beale."

"Well, Charlie, first of all, the dog didn't bite your boy, although no one would have blamed him if he had, seeing as how that little snot was poking the dog with a stick."

"Who are you calling a little snot?" he growled.

"Sorry, my mistake. He's clearly a very big snot."

"I want compensation."

"For what? Being ugly and stupid? I'm not sure they pay out for that."

"You think you're smart, don't you?"

"I have my moments. Now, was there something else I can help you with?"

"Where's the dog?"

"I left him at home."

"That's him, Dad." Toerag Junior pointed down the park. "The black one."

"Right." The man pulled out a small metal bar, which he must have had hidden down the back of his trousers.

"No, you don't." I stepped in front of him to block his path.

"Get out of my way!" He put out his hands to try to push me away. That didn't quite work out for him because moments later, he was on his backside, looking slightly startled. When he'd recovered, he reached out to pick up the metal bar that he'd dropped, but I kicked it away, and put my foot on his hand. "Ouch! Get off me! That's assault. I could have you arrested for that."

"Why don't you call the police? I'm sure they'd be interested to hear why you were carrying this weapon."

He got to his feet. "You haven't heard the last of this."

"Aren't you going to get the dog, Dad?" Toerag Junior bleated.

"Later. Come on." The man grabbed the kid, and the two of them hurried out of the gates.

Moments later, Luke came charging back up the park; Rexy was doing his best to keep up with him.

"What happened, Kat? I saw the man on the ground."

"He tripped."

"He's not going to have Rexy put down, is he?"

"No, of course not. There's nothing for you to worry about."

"Does that mean I can take Rexy for a walk by myself next time?"

"I might just come with you for a few more days."

"Why?"

"Here's a tip for later life. When a girl says she wants to spend time with you, you don't ask her why."

"Girls are stupid."

***

On the one hand, this was the first 'date' I'd been on for

ages, so I thought maybe I should get dressed up. On the other hand, it was at the Gerbil, and no one ever got dressed up to go to the Gerbil.

Except for Graham, apparently.

"You look very grand, City Boy."

"Thanks. It's not too late to go somewhere else."

"What? After I got dressed up specially?"

"You were wearing those same clothes earlier."

"I see you made an effort. Where did you get the aftershave from? The seventies store?"

"Don't you like it?"

"Yeah, it's okay. I reckon my granddad used to have some just like that."

He led the way inside and found us a quiet table — it wasn't difficult — most of them were vacant.

"I'll go and get a couple of menus," he said.

"Okay." Good luck with that.

Moments later, he was back. "They don't have a menu."

"Really?" I grinned.

"Why didn't you tell me?"

"I didn't think you'd believe me. I'm going to have the scampi."

"I was hoping for pasta."

"You're bang out of luck, then."

"I'm not sure that bird should be allowed in here." Graham clearly wasn't impressed by Billy, the parrot.

"It's okay, he's had his claws clipped. Have you made up your mind what you're having yet? I'm starving."

"I suppose I'll have the same as you. Will someone come over to take our order?"

"What do you think?"

"Right. I'd better go to the bar, then."

While we waited for the food to arrive, Graham did his best to make small talk.

"Tell me about your work," he said. "Isn't it dangerous?"

"Not really. Most of the time, it's pretty boring. How was your day?"

"Same old, same old. Being a lawyer can be pretty boring."

"It made a change not to see you in the park earlier."

"How come you were in there? Was Luke AWOL again?"

"No, but I thought I ought to go with him in case Little Toerag's dad showed up."

"*Little Toerag* being the kid who attacked the dog, I assume? Were they there?"

"They were. And not a brain cell between them."

"What happened?"

"We had a friendly little chat."

"And?"

"He said he wanted compensation for the kid's chewed arm. And I told him to do one."

"What did he say to that?"

"Nothing really. He tripped in the mud, and then the two of them went home."

"Why do I get the feeling that you aren't telling me everything?"

"Because you're a lawyer, and lawyers don't trust anything anyone says."

"You've had a lot of experience of working with lawyers, have you?"

"Enough to have seen them help a lot of nasty people

walk away from the courts scot-free, when they should have been locked up."

"Better ten guilty people are set free than one innocent person is wrongly convicted."

"Try telling that to the old lady who got mugged, and saw her attacker walk away on a technicality."

He took a deep breath. "Maybe we should change the subject."

"Sure. What about those Hammers?"

"Are you a football fan?"

"No, I can't stand the game. You?"

"I prefer rugby and cricket."

"Of course you do. And tennis, I bet. Or squash."

"I don't know where you get the idea that I'm posh. What sports are you into?"

"I used to do judo when I was a kid, and I still go kick-boxing when I get the chance."

"Remind me not to upset you. What about team sports?"

"I played for the local darts team once back in Leeds. Does that count?"

"Are you ever serious about anything?"

"Not if I can help it."

Our sparkling conversation was interrupted when Kenny brought over the scampi and chips.

"I've not seen this young man of yours in here before, Kat. Aren't you going to introduce me?"

"No. Where's the salt and vinegar?"

"It's over there." He huffed. "Help yourself."

"You were a bit rude to him, weren't you?" Graham said, in a hushed voice.

"You should be thanking me. If I'd given him an opening, he'd have pulled up a chair, and we'd have been stuck with him for the next half-hour."

"These are hot." Graham was trying desperately not to spit out the chip that was melting the skin off the roof of his mouth.

"Sorry, I should have warned you. Becky cooks them in a blast furnace."

By the time we'd finished our meal, the pub was much busier.

"I didn't realise this place did so well." Graham glanced around.

"Most of them are here for the card games. And I don't mean Bridge."

"Is that legal?"

"Always the lawyer." I grinned. "You can't help yourself, can you?"

"I was just thinking out loud. Do you ever play?"

"No, I've got better things to do with my money. Like pay the rent, and on a good week, buy food."

"Things can't be that bad, surely?"

"There's no monthly salary, medical insurance or pension in my line of work."

"If it's so bad, why don't you change jobs?"

"Because I love what I do. I could never work in a shop or an office. I'd be climbing the walls before the first day was out."

Chapter 16

One of the things I hated most about first dates—not that I'd had that many of them—was the awkward ritual that inevitably followed. To kiss goodnight or not to kiss goodnight.

I'd enjoyed Graham's company, and unless I'd totally misread the signs (it wouldn't be the first time), he'd enjoyed the evening too. But now we were standing outside the Gerbil, both of us waiting for the other one to make the first move. Or not, as the case may be.

Then, out of the blue, he did something totally unexpected: He yelled, "Kat!"

It seemed like a strange thing to do, seeing as I was literally three feet away, looking straight at him. Even stranger, he put his hands on my shoulders and threw me to the ground. Now, I have to be honest, I've been out with a few weirdos in my time, but none of them had wrestled me to the ground in the street.

If I'd seen it coming, my judo instincts would have kicked in, and he would have been the one on his back. But seriously, who expects their date to act like that?

Before I could ask him what he was playing at, I realised he'd thrown himself onto the ground too, but not quickly enough to dodge the car that had mounted the pavement. It clipped him on the leg, throwing him against the pub's doors.

"Graham!" I leapt to my feet, and rushed over to him. "Are you okay?"

Yes, I do realise it was a stupid question.

"I'm okay," he said before losing consciousness.

"Graham!"

By now, several of the Gerbil's customers had come outside to see what was happening.

"I've called an ambulance." A woman with a glass of beer in her hand stepped forward. "Is he okay?"

"I don't know."

He was still breathing, and the only injuries I could see were those to his right leg, which looked broken, and a gash on the side of his face. But who knew what internal injuries he might have sustained? Graham must have seen the car, and pushed me clear of its path.

The car? Where was the car?

I looked down the road, but there was no sign of it.

***

I wasn't allowed to travel with him in the ambulance, and by the time I'd flagged down a taxi, the blue sirens had long since disappeared. He could have been taken to any one of three hospitals, and as Sod's law would have it, I drew a blank at the first two.

"Are you a relative?" The fearsome woman behind reception at the third hospital barked at me.

"Err, yeah, I'm his sister."

She checked the screen. "He's in surgery."

"What for?"

"According to this, he has a broken tibia and fibula."

"Anything else?"

"Concussion. That's all I have down here."

"When will I be able to see him?"

"If you take a seat over there, someone will call you. What's your name?"

"Kat Royle."

Hospital waiting rooms are the worst. Three hours and four cups of what masqueraded as coffee later, I was practically climbing the walls.

"Kat Royle?"

"That's me." I hurried over to the nurse who'd called my name. "How is he? Can I see him?"

"He's okay, but he's still quite drowsy. It might be better to come back in the morning."

"I'm going away tomorrow," I lied. "Could I just see him for a few minutes now?"

"Okay, but it'll have to be very quick."

She directed me to Pullman Ward, which was on the second floor. Graham's leg was in plaster, but other than that, he looked okay. He appeared to be asleep.

"One minute, and then you have to go," the nurse reminded me before leaving us alone.

I waited until she had left the ward. "Graham, are you awake?"

"Kat?" He opened one eye. "Are you okay?"

"I'm fine, thanks to you. How's the leg?"

"It feels okay at the moment, but I suspect it's going to hurt like hell when the happy juice wears off."

"What about your head?"

"A bit of a headache but it's nothing."

"You saved my life."

"Did I? I don't remember very much about it."

"If you hadn't pushed me out of the way of that car, I'd have been a goner."

"Does that mean you'll go out with me again?"

"Not if it's going to end like it did this time."

"What happened to the driver of the car?"

"He didn't stop."

"Was it an accident?"

"I don't know. Probably some kid, joy-riding, who lost control."

"Time's up!" The nurse was back. "You have to leave now."

"Couldn't she stay a little longer?" Graham said.

"Sorry, no, but your sister can visit you tomorrow."

Graham gave me a puzzled look and mouthed, "*Sister?*"

"See you tomorrow, bro." I gave him a peck on the cheek, and then started to follow the nurse out of the ward. Suddenly, something occurred to me. "Graham, what about Miles?"

"I'll call my Dad. He'll pick him up and take him to Canterbury."

"I can see to the dog if you like?"

"It's okay. I'm going to be out of action for some weeks. Dad loves dogs. Miles will be spoiled while he's there."

"You have to leave now!" the nurse was rapidly losing her patience.

"Sorry. Coming."

Despite what I'd said to Graham, I didn't think the incident had been an accident or joy-riders. Someone had tried to take me out, and if it hadn't been for Graham's prompt actions, they may very well have succeeded.

A pattern was beginning to emerge. First Roy. Then Westy. And now me. This had to be related to one of the cases that Roy and/or Westy had been working on, but to figure out what that might be, I needed to find those accounts.

By the time I left the hospital, it was almost two in the morning. The tube and buses weren't an option, so I took a taxi back to my flat. Between the two taxis that day, I'd spent another hundred pounds of the cash that Vi had given me.

***

It was almost eleven o'clock the next morning when I finally found the energy to drag myself out of bed. Good thing it was Saturday.

Once I was dressed, I called at the Widow Manning's.

"You look terrible," she greeted me.

"Thanks. I just wanted to check that Luke didn't have any trouble in the park this morning. I had planned to go with him, but I overslept."

"He didn't mention anything to me."

"Did he seem okay?"

"I think so. That young man never has much to say for himself."

"Okay, thanks."

Back in the flat, I called the hospital. Graham had apparently had a comfortable night, and was expected to be discharged later that afternoon. I said I'd be there to pick him up.

In the Gerbil, Kenny seemed unconcerned that Billy was nibbling at his ear.

"How's that boyfriend of yours, Kat?"

"He's got a broken leg, but he'll be out of hospital this afternoon. Graham isn't my boyfriend, though."

"If you say so. Nasty business that yesterday. I had the Old Bill around here this morning. Have they caught up with you yet?"

"No, but I suppose they could have called while I was still in bed. I doubt I'd have heard them. What did they have to say?"

"Not much. It was a young copper, still a bit wet behind the ears. He wanted to know if anyone had seen what happened."

"That's what I came in to ask you. What did you tell him?"

"That I didn't think so. First we knew about it was when we heard your boyfriend—sorry—your *friend* crash into the door. Didn't you see who was driving?"

"No, I had my back to the car. If Graham hadn't pushed me out of the way, it would have been curtains for me, I reckon."

"You must have got a look at the car when it drove off?"

"Only a glimpse. It was small—red. A Corsa maybe, but I couldn't swear to it. I didn't see the plates."

"The copper asked me to stick up a notice in case anyone saw anything. Becky is going to get some printed on the computer. What do you reckon, Kat? Joy-riders? There's been a few of them around here recently."

"Yeah, probably. Do me a favour, would you, Kenny? If anyone comes forward to say they saw something, get them to call me."

"Sure." He took a notepad and pen from underneath the counter. "Scribble your number on here."

Once I was back outside, I called Bruce Layne.

"Bruce, it's Kat."

"Are you feeling okay?"

"How did you hear about it?"

"Hear about what?"

"You just asked if I was okay, so I assumed you must have heard about my little incident yesterday."

"I asked if you were okay because that's the first time you've not called me Batman. What little incident are we talking about?"

I told him what had happened outside the Gerbil, and of my suspicions that it may not have been an accident.

"And you say one of our lads was over at the Gerbil earlier today?"

"Yeah. According to Kenny, it was a young plod."

"You have such a way with words, Kat."

"Is there any chance you could check it out? If you could trace the car, that would be great."

"And how am I supposed to do that?"

"There are CCTV cameras on the road."

"I can't make any promises, but I'll see what our guys have done so far."

"You're a superstar, Batman."

"Shouldn't that be a superhero?"

***

Graham was waiting for me in the ward, seated in a wheelchair.

"Hey, Hopalong, how are you doing?"

"Is that my new nickname? What about City Boy?"

"You'll revert to that when the leg is mended. Did they say how long it will be?"

"Six to eight weeks they reckon. I wanted to go down to

reception, but they wouldn't let me leave until someone came to collect me."

"It's just as well I didn't have something better to do then, isn't it?"

"Can you grab those?" He pointed to a pair of crutches under the bed.

Once we were in the lift, he looked at me, grinned and shook his head.

"What?"

"I've been on a few first dates, but I have to say this one is the most eventful so far."

"Who said it was a *date*?" I said, with mock indignance.

"Sorry, I—err, I just meant—"

"Actually, I was just about to ask you back to my place for coffee last night when the car intervened."

"Really?" His face lit up.

"No, I just said that to see your reaction." I grinned. "Did the police come to see you?"

"Yes. A young police officer interviewed me this morning."

"Probably the same one who went to the Gerbil."

"I couldn't really tell him anything."

"You must have got a good look at the car before you pushed me out of its path?"

"It's all a bit of a blur. I remember that we were talking, and then the next thing I remember, I was in the ambulance. Did you see who was driving?"

"No. I barely saw the car. Like I said yesterday, it was most likely joy-riders."

"You can put me in a taxi now. I'll be fine from here."

"No chance. I want to see where you live."

"Why?"

"So I can have a laugh at your soft furnishings."

I'd always assumed Graham lived in Lewford, but the address he gave the taxi driver was actually in Greenwich.

"I thought you said you lived in Lewford?"

"I never said that. You just assumed I did."

"How come you're always hanging around Lewford, then?"

"It's only just up the road, and Miles enjoys the walk. Plus, the company's better."

Fortunately, for all concerned, his flat was on the ground floor.

Much as I would have liked to rip the piss out of his furnishings, I couldn't. The living room looked like it belonged in a show flat.

"Welcome to my humble abode." He was slowly getting used to walking on the crutches.

"If you think this is humble, I'm never inviting you to my place. Did the furniture come with the flat?"

"No. I chose it all."

"This place is enormous."

"If you think this is big, you should have seen the apartment I had in Limehouse."

"It must have been posh if you're calling it an *apartment*. I thought you said NGO lawyers didn't get paid well?"

"Compared to lawyers working in private practice, they don't."

"But compared to the rest of us mere mortals, you're minted."

"Would you like coffee?"

"Yeah, but I'll make it. Please tell me your kitchen is a mess, at least."

"It is. I didn't get around to putting the dishes in the dishwasher yesterday."

Graham's idea of *a mess* and mine were several light years apart. The spacious kitchen was spotless, and equipped with every gadget known to man.

"Where's your kettle?" I shouted.

"There's a coffee machine to the left of the window."

"Of course there is." I studied it for a few minutes. "Nope, no idea how this thing works."

He hobbled into the kitchen. "I have decaf pods if you'd prefer?" He pointed to one of the cupboards.

"I didn't even realise you could get coffee in pods. Mine comes in a jar."

We settled down in the living room: me on the sofa, Graham in the matching armchair.

"What will you do about work?" I took a sip of the coffee.

"I'll probably take a few days off until I'm comfortable on the crutches. I can work from home anyway."

"I'm sorry about what happened. It wasn't the ideal end to the date."

His face lit up. "You just called it a date?"

"I meant *meal*."

"Yes, but you actually said *date*."

"Slip of the tongue."

We chatted for an hour or so, by which time I could tell he was beginning to flag.

"I'd better get going." I took the cups through to the kitchen. "Give me a call if you need anything."

"I don't have your number."

"Give me your phone." I added my number to his contacts and handed it back.

"When will I see you again?"

"I'll give you a call on Monday to see how you're doing."

"And to arrange a second date?"

"We haven't had a first one yet."

Chapter 17

By the time I got back to Lewford, it was almost five o'clock. After the hectic last couple of days, I planned to spend a quiet night in. But first, I had to get something to eat. So far today, all I'd had was the stale sandwich I'd managed to grab at the hospital, and a few biscuits at Graham's. I'd offered to stay and make him something to eat, but he was out on his feet or should that be foot? He wanted to get some sleep before he ate anything.

I had a craving for fish and chips.

I loved living in London, but one of the biggest disappointments had been the scarcity of chippies. Up north, where I came from, you couldn't move for them. And the few there were down here weren't what I'd call a 'real' chippy. If they didn't get their curry, gravy and peas delivered by the barrel, then they weren't the real deal. And, needless to say, they had to sell pickled eggs. Don't even get me started on what passes for a fishcake down here.

Fortunately, though, the real McCoy was to be found less than half a mile from my flat. Martha's Plaice wasn't quite up to northern standards (I had to deduct a few points for their fishcakes), but they were as close as you could get down here.

"Hey, Kat." Martha was dipping a fish into batter. "Long time no see. I thought you'd defected to the competition."

"Like who? You're the only decent chippy for miles."

"Your usual?"

"Yes, please." My usual was cod, chips and mushy peas. Haddock at a push.

"Open or wrapped?"

"Open, please."

Mmm! I'm pretty sure I'd sell my soul for a serving of fish, chips and peas.

"Giz a chip, Mrs," some cheeky youngster shouted as I walked along the high street.

"Buy your own." I might have given him one, but he'd blown his chances as soon as he made the mistake of calling me *Mrs*.

I'd almost eaten up by the time I reached Walt's house. The For Sale sign now read: Sold. I wasn't surprised. Properties around here got snapped up as soon as they came onto the market. No doubt someone would convert the house into three or four flats and make a killing.

I'd just put the empty fish and chip carton in the bin, and was looking forward to getting home, and streaming a box set on Netflix when my phone rang.

"Kat, it's Christine." She was the last person I wanted to hear from right then.

"Hi."

"Ralph's just called to say he's going to work late again."

"It's Saturday."

"You said to call the next time he did it."

"Right." Me and my big mouth.

"Where are you now? Will you be able to follow him?"

"Yeah, I guess so. I'd better get a move on, though."

"Okay, thanks."

Although I was disappointed not to be going home to an evening's mindless TV, I was only too aware that I needed to bring in some cash. I wasn't in a position to turn down any more work. It had been painful enough having to drop out of the Premax case.

Even though I sprinted to the betting shop, I only just made it there in time. Ralph was turning the corner as I arrived, so I had to nip into the same newsagents to avoid being spotted by him.

"The new edition of Trains and Tracks Monthly came in yesterday." The man behind the counter was still rocking the string vest look.

"Right." I was much more interested in keeping tracks on Ralph.

"Do you want it?"

"Err — no, thanks. I've given up on the trains." I made my exit and started down the street after my mark.

Just as on the previous occasion, he headed for the tube station, so once again, I tucked in at the far end of the same carriage. I was expecting him to get off at Mudchute, and I'd almost committed to exiting the train when I realised that he hadn't got up from his seat.

Where was he going this time?

He left the train at Heron Quays, and from there, sprinted the short distance to Canary Wharf where he took the Jubilee Line. Fifteen minutes later, he changed again, this time at Green Park, onto the Piccadilly line. By now, I was beginning to wonder if he knew he was being followed, and was leading me a merry dance. At South Kensington, he set off on foot at a fast pace. A few minutes later, he reached his destination: The Royal Marsden Hospital.

I saw him go through the main entrance, but then I'd made the fatal mistake of stopping to catch my breath. In those few seconds, I managed to lose sight of him. I was furious with myself. I'd just spent the best part of an hour following him, and now I had no idea where he was. It would have been pointless to wander around the hospital because he could have been anywhere, and there was very little likelihood of my spotting him. Instead, I took a seat in reception, in the hope that he'd come out the same way as he'd gone in.

While flicking through a two-year old copy of House and Garden, my phone beeped with a text from Christine, asking if I had any news. I didn't reply. What would I have told her? That I'd lost him again?

I'd been there for almost two hours. My backside was numb, and I was pretty sure that I'd blown it, but then Ralph reappeared. He was with a woman who I recognised from the photograph Zero had sent me when he was staking out the flat in the Isle of Dogs; it was Deborah Todman. That kind of made sense. She must have recovered from whatever had been ailing her, and Ralph had come to collect her.

I still found it hard to understand why he would cheat on Christine with a woman almost thirty years older, but I'd long since given up trying to understand men.

I needed to position myself somewhere that I'd be able to snap a photo of them together. Once I'd passed the incriminating photo on to Christine, that would be case closed as far as I was concerned. Unfortunately, the reception area was so busy that it was difficult to get a clear snap of them.

I moved in a little closer until I had the perfect angle. I was just about to take the shot when I saw something that stopped me dead in my tracks. They were both sobbing.

That completely threw me, and I was still trying to

recover myself when—

"Kat?" Ralph said. "Is that you?"

Well done, Kat! That was just brilliant. The shock of seeing them in such obvious distress had thrown me off my guard, and now I'd allowed him to see me.

"Oh? Hi, Ralph."

He said something to the woman who then went and took a seat.

"Are you visiting someone?" He wiped a tear from his eye.

"Yeah, something like that. Look, I don't want to keep you. I can see you're upset."

"It's okay. Can I ask you a favour?"

"Err, sure."

"I know you don't like me."

"I wouldn't say that."

"It's okay. The way I treated Chrissy back then was unforgiveable."

"With Fiona, you mean?"

"Yes." He bowed his head, and to my surprise, he began to cry again. "I'm sorry about this."

"Don't worry about it. Look, Ralph, I think I should tell you what I'm—"

"She's dead." He wiped his eyes again. "Fiona's dead."

"Oh? I—err—"

"That's her mother, Deborah, over there. I arrived here twenty minutes too late."

"I'm really sorry."

"Can I ask you a massive favour, Kat? If you see Chrissy again, please don't tell her about any of this."

"Well, I—err—"

"There hasn't been anything going on between me and

Fiona, I promise. Not since that time when you caught me. Back then, I realised what a fool I was, and how close I'd come to losing Chrissy, so I ended it. I've never looked at another woman since. On my life."

"So how come you're here now?"

"That's Fiona's mum." He gestured to Deborah. "She contacted me a few weeks ago, to tell me that Fiona was terminally ill. Cancer. She only had a few weeks to live. According to Deborah, Fiona had never met anyone else after we split up. Apparently, she still talked about me from time to time, so Deborah asked if I'd mind paying her a visit."

"Did you tell Christine?"

"No. I was worried about how she might react."

"You should have told her. If Christine had known all the facts, she would have understood."

"You're probably right. I wasn't thinking straight. It's too late now, though. If you do see Chrissy, please don't say anything, Kat. I couldn't bear the thought of losing her."

"Okay. I won't say a word."

"Thanks. I'd better take Deborah home."

***

I made a call to Christine.

"Kat? I've been trying to get hold of you. What's happening?"

"Where are you now?"

"I'm at home. Why?"

"I need to come and talk to you."

"What's happened? Why can't you tell me over the

phone?"

"I need to do this face to face."

"Oh God. It's bad, isn't it? I knew he was cheating on me. Where is the scumbag?"

"Listen to me, Christine. It's not bad, I promise, but I need to talk to you before Ralph gets home."

"Okay." I could hear the tears in her voice.

"Text me your address, and I'll be there as quick as I can."

The train would have taken too long, so I took a taxi to Deborah's flat. The fare plus tip cost me just over sixty quid, which I paid out of what remained of the cash that Vi had given me.

Christine's house in Purley was a mid-terraced property with a front garden the size of a postage stamp. Christine was watching for me through the front window, and had opened the front door before I got to it.

"What's going on, Kat?" Her eyes were red and puffy.

I spent the next ten minutes telling her everything I knew. I honestly had no idea how she was going to react.

"She's died?" Christine grabbed the box of tissues.

"Yeah. Ralph and her mother were leaving the hospital when I bumped into them."

"He should have told me."

"He was worried about how you'd react. After all, she was the woman he'd had an affair with."

"I would have understood under the circumstances."

"Are you sure about that?"

"I'd like to think so, but probably not." She managed a half-hearted laugh. "What did he say when he saw you? He doesn't know that you were following him, does he?"

"No."

"Are you sure?"

"I'm certain. His head was all over the place. He just assumed my being there was a coincidence. He was worried that I might tell you, though."

"What did you say?"

"That I wouldn't breathe a word of it."

"Where is he now?"

"He's taking Fiona's mother home to the Isle of Dogs."

"What do you think I should do, Kat?"

"That's not my call."

"I know, but I'd still appreciate your advice."

"I suppose that depends on if you still love him or not. And whether or not you want to continue in this relationship."

"I still love him. I can't help myself."

"In that case, it seems to me you have two choices. Either you pretend you don't know about any of this, and carry on as normal. Or you tell him that you know about Fiona, and that you understand why he did what he did."

"But that would mean I'd have to tell him that I hired you to follow him. What will he think once he knows that?"

"He doesn't have to know that. You can just say I called you out of the blue. Make out I did it out of spite."

"That doesn't seem fair on you."

"Why? Because Ralph will think badly of me? I can live with that."

"What if he comes back while you're still here?" She hurried to the window, and looked up and down the street.

"I think he'll be a while yet. Fiona's mother was in a

pretty bad way. I'd better get going, anyway."

"Thanks, Kat." She gave me a hug. "I'm sorry I was such a cow to you for so long."

"Forget it."

"We'll stay in touch, yeah?"

"Sure."

"What about your bill? You can't send it to the house in case Ralph sees it."

"I can text you with the amount if you like?"

"Yes, please. And is it okay if I pay in cash? I don't want Ralph to see anything on the bank statement."

"Cash will be fine."

The cost of the taxi journey from the hospital to Christine's house would be included on her bill, but I couldn't in all conscience justify taking another one to get back home. Instead, I was forced to endure a forty-five minute train journey via London Bridge.

By the time I arrived back at the flat, it was after eleven, and I had just about enough strength to climb into bed.

Chapter 18

It was Sunday morning; my favourite day of the week.

I'd set the alarm, so I'd be up in time to go to the park with Luke and Rexy. Needless to say, the young lad wasn't too impressed that he had to put up with my company again.

It turned out to be another no-show from Mr Beale, so I promised Luke I'd let him walk Rexy alone from then on. I could only assume that Toerag Senior had decided that being embarrassed in front of his son once was enough.

Back at the flat, I was debating what to do about breakfast when my phone rang.

"Zero? What's up?"

"I didn't wake you, did I, Kat?"

"Course not. I've been up for ages. Is something the matter?"

"No. Toyah had to work this weekend, so I took a look at the Premax CCTV yesterday."

"You must have been really bored if that's the most exciting thing you could come up with to pass the time."

"I like this kind of stuff."

"How on earth did you ever get a girlfriend? And why bother with the Premax tape? I've dropped that case."

"I know, but I just thought I'd take a look anyway. There's something I think you should see."

"What?"

"I can't really explain over the phone. I thought if you weren't doing anything today, we could meet at the office."

"What makes you think I'm not doing anything? I'll

have you know I have a hectic social calendar."

"Oh? Okay, then."

"Zero, wait. I was only kidding. There's something I need to talk to you about anyway. I was going to do it tomorrow, but I guess we could get together today. It'll give me an excuse to get breakfast at Joe's. I might even treat you to a full English if you ask nicely."

"That's okay. I've already had some Shredded Wheat."

"Yummy, yummy. Lucky you." I checked my watch. "How about I see you at the office at eleven? That'll give me time to grab breakfast first."

"Okay. See you later."

Wow! I certainly couldn't knock that young man's work ethic. When I was his age, I didn't realise that Sunday mornings even existed. The Premax thing was a waste of time, but I wanted to update him on Christine Mather's case, and also to tell him about what happened to Graham. If I was right that I'd been targeted because of something Roy or Westy was working on, it was just possible Zero could be in danger too.

***

"Is your calendar fast or something, Kat?" Joe was by himself behind the counter in the cafe. "It's not Monday, you know."

"No rest for the wicked. It's quiet in here. I'm surprised you bother opening on a Sunday."

"If I didn't, I'd have to spend time at home with the missus. What are you doing here today, anyway?"

"I'm just on my way into the office. I thought I'd treat

myself to one of your full English specials first."

"You're out of luck. It's just toast or cereals on a Sunday."

"What? Crap!"

"I'm just messing with you. Do you want brown or white toast with your breakfast?"

"White, please."

"What's happening to the business now that your boss has gone and got himself murdered?"

"I've taken over. I'm going to keep the place going if I can."

"Good for you."

Ten minutes later, my full English was on the table.

"Did that fella catch up with you yesterday, Kat? The guy with the bushy sideburns?"

"No. Did he say what he wanted?"

"No. He said he'd been to your offices but there was no one in. I told him to try again tomorrow."

"Okay, thanks."

Zero was already at his desk when I arrived.

"Shredded Wheat?" I shook my head. "Seriously?"

"Toyah reckons they're good for you."

"It could be worse. It could be muesli. Let's go through to my office."

Zero was keen to get started. "The first time I watched the CCTV footage, I didn't—"

"Whoa! Have you forgotten something?"

"Coffee?"

"Correct. And make it strong. By rights, I shouldn't even be out of bed at this time on a Sunday morning."

He only made the one cup because he'd brought a bottle

of water in for himself.

"Shall I show you what I found on the CCTV?" He grabbed the mouse.

"In a minute. I need to tell you a couple of things before we get started on that. First, I've wrapped up the Christine Mather case, so I need you to prepare the bill." I fished into my pocket and produced the receipt for the taxi. "Make sure you add that in."

"What happened?"

I told him all about Ralph and Fiona, and my trip to the hospital. "And, I remembered to log it all in TimeLogMaster. Aren't you impressed?"

"Surprised, more like."

"Cheeky sod."

"What's Christine going to do?"

"I'm not absolutely sure, but I'd guess she won't say anything to him. She'll just carry on as if nothing ever happened."

"How will she explain away our bill?"

"Oh, yeah. It's a good job you mentioned that. Don't post it to her whatever you do. Let me have it, and I'll text her the details. She'll be paying by cash."

"It doesn't sound like you had much of a break yesterday."

"You haven't heard the half of it."

I told him what had happened outside the Gerbil, and about my other visit to the hospital.

"And you reckon the guy in the car was trying to hit you?"

"Positive. First Roy, then Westy and now me. It's too much of a coincidence. Whoever it is must think we have the file that Roy and Westy were working on."

"But we don't have it."

"Yeah, but they don't know that. We're both going to have to be on our guard."

"Me?" He clearly hadn't seen that coming.

"You're most likely not in any danger, but better safe than sorry."

"Do I get danger money?"

"If you'd gone with me to Joe's, I'd have stood you a full English, but you blew me off for a couple of Shredded Wheat."

"Don't you think you ought to tell the police that someone tried to kill you?"

"I have. Sort of, anyway." I finished off the last of the coffee. "Let's take a look at what you found on the CCTV."

A few clicks of the mouse later, and we were viewing the CCTV footage taken from Premax.

"This is from inside the loading bay," Zero said.

"I recognise it."

He pointed to the screen. "Watch that door."

I did as he said, and moments later, it opened, and in walked me and the rest of the cleaning crew.

"Those overalls don't get any better." He laughed.

"Less of the cheek."

"Keep watching."

On screen, I and the other cleaners had left the loading bay, and disappeared from view. After that, there was nothing much to see.

"What am I supposed to be looking for?" I asked.

"There! It just happened."

"*What* just happened? I didn't see anything."

"I'll play it again from the point where you and the others disappear, but this time I'm going to zoom in on that section of wall between the door and the loading bay gate."

"O-kay?"

He reran the footage, but this time all I saw was the wall.

"If this is some kind of wind-up —?"

"You're not watching closely enough." He rewound it again, but this time played it at a much slower speed. After a few seconds, he pointed. "Do you see that?"

I had to strain to see what he was pointing at. "That black mark?"

"It isn't a mark." He zoomed in even closer.

"A spider?"

"Bingo."

"So what?"

"Keep watching."

I was just about to tear a strip off him for wasting my time when —

"It jumped!" I yelled.

"Have you ever known a spider to jump?"

"Certainly not like that one just did."

One moment, the spider had been walking in a straight line across the wall, and the next, it was on the other side of the screen, almost out of frame.

"Do you realise what that means?" Zero was clearly excited about something, but I didn't have the first clue what.

"Not really."

"Someone has edited the tape."

"What about the timestamp?"

"The timestamp doesn't show a gap, but there must be one otherwise how did the spider get from there to there?"

"So you're saying that someone has deliberately doctored the footage by removing a section?"

"Yes. There can't be much missing, so whatever happened must have taken place very quickly."

"Immediately after we'd entered the building?"

"Correct."

"But isn't there a camera focussed on the outside of that door?"

"There is, and the footage from that camera doesn't show anything untoward. My guess would be they doctored that too, but there's no spider there for me to check it with."

"If what you're saying is correct, then whoever is operating their CCTV must be in on this too?"

"Definitely."

"Zero, you're a genius."

"I like to think so. What are you going to do?"

"I don't know. I'll need to have a think about it."

"There's something else I wanted to tell you, Kat. I think I've tracked down Lisa."

"Seriously?"

"Yeah. Well, to be more precise, I've tracked down her phone."

"What's her address? I'll pay her a visit."

"It might not be as simple as all that."

"Why not?"

"If I'm right, and I think I am, she's in a hotel close to Waterloo station."

"Room number?"

"I'm good, but I'm not that good. I can't pinpoint the phone to a specific room. Not from here, anyway."

"Fair enough. What's the hotel?"

"Waterloo Gardens. It has over three hundred rooms."

"Right. That's not great but it's more than we had before."

"I could go to the hotel now if you like."

"And do what?"

"See if I can figure out which room she's in."

"How will you do that?" He gave me that now familiar look of his. "Let me guess. I don't want to know."

"It's just better that you don't."

"How will you get past reception?"

"It's a budget hotel, so I won't look out of place. There'll be crowds of tourists coming and going all the time. I don't think I'll have any problems."

"Just don't go getting yourself arrested. I'd offer to go with you, but I really ought to go and check on Graham."

"How long have you and he been an item?"

"We aren't. Friday was the first time we'd been out together."

"Wow!" He laughed. "That was some first date."

"It wasn't a *date*. We just grabbed something to eat."

"If you say so."

***

Graham answered the door on his crutches.

"Hey, Hopalong, how are you doing?"

"Not bad. I think I'm slowly getting the hang of these things. I wasn't expecting to see you today."

"I just thought I ought to—"

"Graham!" The female voice came from inside the flat. "Was that the door?"

The next moment, a leggy blonde wearing a tad too much make-up appeared at his side.

"Err, Kat, this is Sharon. Sharon this is Kat Royle."

She stepped forward, all smiles and ringlets, and offered her hand. "Hi. Pleased to meet you."

"Likewise."

"Sharon just popped over to see how I was doing," Graham said.

"That was very kind of her."

"Did you hear what happened to him?" Sharon said. "Poor little love."

"Skydiving, wasn't it?" I raised an eyebrow at Graham.

"No, he got knocked down by a car." Sharon corrected me.

"Really? That's terrible."

"Kat's just joking," Graham said. "She was with me when it happened."

"Oh?" Sharon gave me a closer look. "I didn't realise."

"Anyway." I took a step back. "I can't stay. I just wanted to check that you were okay."

"Thanks for coming over, Kat," Graham said.

"Yeah, thanks—err—" She stumbled on my name.

"Kat."

"Don't worry about Graham. I'll make sure he's okay."

"Great. Bye, then."

What was it with me and men? How did I always end up picking losers, cheats or liars?

I'd just exited the building when someone shouted my name.

"Kat!" Graham came hobbling after me.

"Slow down. You'll do yourself an injury."

"I didn't want you to leave before I'd had the chance to explain."

"There's nothing to explain. I only came over to check that you were okay, and you clearly are."

"I had no idea that Sharon was going to come over."

"I think it's sweet that you two have stayed in touch."

"We haven't. Not really."

"Just the occasional conjugal visit, then?"

"No, nothing like that, I swear. This is the first time she's been here, honestly. Her mother works at the hospital where I was admitted. She told Sharon that she'd seen me. I had no idea she was coming over until she turned up this morning."

"Right. I still have to get going."

"Before you do." He hobbled a little closer. "I was going to do this the other night. Before I was hit by that car." He leaned forward, and planted a kiss on my lips. "I really would like to see you again, Kat. What do you say?"

"Maybe, provided that you don't bring Sharon."

"I won't. I promise."

Chapter 19

The next morning, at a quarter past six, I was having the best dream. I was in a deckchair on a beach somewhere, next to a clear blue ocean. I was drinking a cocktail while being serenaded by a handsome man, playing a Spanish guitar.

When my phone rang and dragged me back to reality, I was not best pleased.

"What?" I yelled.

"It's me, Kat." Zero had spent the night at the Waterloo Gardens hotel.

"Sorry. Morning, Zero. Was your room okay?"

"It's great. This is the first time I've ever stayed in a real hotel."

"Don't be ridiculous."

"It's true. I've stayed in lots of B&Bs and a few AirBnBs, but never in a proper hotel."

Tragic.

The previous night, Zero had contacted me to confirm he'd identified which room Lisa was staying in. There'd been no sign of her by ten o'clock, so I'd told him to go home, and return the next day. He'd been the one who'd pointed out he'd be able to make an earlier start if he stayed there, and it wouldn't be much more expensive than the taxi fares home and back. The client would eventually pick up the tab for it, so I agreed. The actual booking of the room proved to be quite problematic, though. Zero had virtually no cash on him, and didn't possess a debit or credit card. In the end, I'd been forced to make the booking online.

"I take it Lisa is still in the hotel?"

"Yeah. Or at least her phone is."

"What time will you be able to start monitoring her room?"

"I've been watching it for the last half-hour."

"Well done you. Give me a call if you see her. I'll pop over to see you shortly, but there's somewhere I need to check first. I'll call you when I'm outside the hotel."

"Okay. Oh, and Kat—"

"Yeah?"

"Am I okay to get breakfast?"

"Of course you are. Have you got enough cash on you?"

"Yeah. There's a McDonald's just up the road. I'll nip out and get a McMuffin."

"Okay. I'll reimburse you when I see you later."

What a little love. When I'd first agreed to take Zero on, the most I'd hoped for was that he'd be able to handle the admin and bookkeeping that Sheila had looked after. He was already doing so much more than that. The guy was a superstar.

***

Before I contacted Kevin Lockhart at Premax, I needed to check that the last piece of the jigsaw fitted.

Deptford Commercial vehicles carried a wide range of vans and minibuses, and according to their website, they had just the vehicle I was interested in.

"Morning, darling." The guy was classic car salesman: Slicked back hair, faux sheepskin coat and an enormous cigar.

"Morning."

"Got anything in mind? We've just had a new delivery

of small vans."

"I'm actually looking for a minibus."

"You've come to the right place. We've got more than a dozen. Beauties, all of them."

"Can I take a look at that one, please?"

"That's what I like to see: A lady who knows her own mind. Wait there, and I'll get the keys." He disappeared into the office, and returned moments later, keys in hand. "I'm Robbie, by the way. But don't worry, I won't be *robbing* you today." He snorted at his little joke. It was a line that I assumed he repeated to every customer. "What's your name, darling?"

"Cindy."

"After you." He held open the driver's door for me.

"Do you mind if I take a look in the back first?"

"Not at all. Be my guest." He went around to the side of the vehicle and slid open the door.

"Thanks."

"It's a fourteen-seater." He followed me on board. "You won't find one in better condition for the money."

"It's very nice." I walked around to the rear of the bus. "Tell me, Robbie. Are all these models the same inside?"

"How do you mean?"

"The seating arrangement? Are they all the same?"

"Yeah. Identical."

"That's great." I started for the door. "Thanks very much."

"Would you like to go for a test drive?"

"No, thanks. I've seen everything I need."

"Shall we go into the office? I'm sure I can come up with a sweet deal for you."

"Thanks, but no. I've decided I'm going to buy a moped

instead."

"A *moped*?"

"Bye, Robbie. Thanks again."

Mission accomplished, I gave Kevin at Premax a call.

"Kat? I didn't expect to hear from you again."

"I want to run an idea by you."

"Okay?"

"I feel bad about having to drop your case in the way I did, and I'd like another crack at it if you'll agree."

"I'm not really sure there's much point."

"Have you hired anyone else yet?"

"Well, no, I haven't had a chance to yet."

"How about you give me one more week on a no result, no fee basis?"

"I'm not sure."

"Come on, Kevin. What do you have to lose? It'll take you that long to find someone else to take over the case anyway."

"Okay. I guess so."

"Great. If it's okay with you, I'll send a colleague of mine over to your place later today. He'll need access to the loading bay."

"To do what?"

"Plant a camera. It shouldn't take him more than a few minutes."

"We already have CCTV in there."

"I know. Humour me, would you?"

"Okay. What's his name?"

"Ze—err, Smith. Mr Smith. I'll get him to ask for you, shall I?"

"Yeah."

"Great. Thanks, Kevin."

***

Zero's mention of breakfast had left me feeling hungry, so I dropped in at the same McDonald's, and treated myself to a sausage and egg McMuffin. Once I'd washed that down with what was laughingly described as coffee, I made my way over to the hotel.

"Zero, I'm outside. Can you pop down?"

"On my way."

Moments later, he appeared, dressed in jeans and a t-shirt that had Big Ben printed on the front.

"What on earth are you wearing?"

"I thought it would make me look more like a tourist."

"O—kay. Any sign of life?"

"None. No one has gone in or out of the room while I've been here."

"Are you sure she's in there?"

"Her phone is." He shrugged.

"There's somewhere I need you to go."

"What about Lisa?"

"I'll stay here until you get back."

"From where?"

"Premax. I've just spoken to the MD, Kevin Lockhart, and he's expecting you."

"Why am I going there?"

"We need eyes on that loading bay and the adjacent door."

"You want me to stake out the loading bay?"

"No, I want you to plant a camera in there. We need to find out what's really happening in that area."

"What kind of camera?"

"Don't ask me. You're the hacker. I thought you'd have some bright ideas."

"Okay, but I'm going to need some money."

"Take this." I gave him my credit card. "The PIN is 1-2-3-4."

"Please tell me you're joking."

"Of course I'm joking. It's 6-7-3-4."

"6-7-3-4. Got it."

"And you need to make sure none of the workforce see you doing it."

"You don't want much, do you?"

"I have every faith in you. Go on, off you go, and get back here as soon as you've done it."

"Will do."

***

No one challenged me as I walked through reception to the bank of lifts. When the doors opened, I waited for a man, dressed in a grey suit, to step out. His face seemed vaguely familiar. It was somewhere between the first and second floors that I realised how I knew the man.

It was Mike Dale.

When the lift doors opened on the third floor, I immediately hit the button for the ground floor, but the lift had other ideas. The doors closed again, and it continued its ascent. Someone on a higher floor had obviously pressed the call button.

"Morning." On the sixth floor, a jovial elderly man stepped into the lift beside me.

"Morning."

Thankfully, the lift had now begun its descent.

"I'm going to Madame Tussauds today," my fellow traveller informed me. "Have you been there?"

"Err, no."

"I hear it's very good. And then I've booked to go on the Eye this afternoon."

"Very nice."

"Have you —?"

As soon as the doors opened on the ground floor, I sprinted through reception and outside.

There was no sign of Dale.

Although I was furious at myself for having allowed him to walk straight by me, at least now I knew Dale was alive and well. I was fairly sure he would return to the hotel because if he'd been checking out, he would have had luggage, or even just the laptop, with him.

The only thing I could do now was to sit and wait.

I'd always had a low boredom threshold, which wasn't the ideal trait for someone in a job that often required they spend long hours doing nothing but keeping watch. By now, you would have thought I'd be used to it, but it never seemed to get any easier.

It was almost one o'clock, and the McMuffin was a distant memory. I would have liked to nip out for a snack, but I daren't leave reception in case I missed Dale's return. My only option was to pay the extortionate price for the chocolate and crisps in the vending machine in reception.

At just after two o'clock, Zero came back.

"How did you get on?"

"No problem." He gave me a thumbs up, and took out his phone. "Look."

On screen was a video showing the view inside the loading bay at Premax. It was the first time I'd actually seen the main loading bay door open.

"Did you have any problems?"

"Of course not. Piece of cake."

"Good man. Can I view this on my phone?"

"Yeah. Check your email. I've already sent you a link."

"You, sir, are going to get a pay rise."

"For real?"

"Absolutely."

"Cool. Have you seen Lisa?"

"No, but I did see Mike Dale."

"Dale? Where is he now?"

"I—err, don't actually know." I had no choice but to swallow my pride, and admit to Zero that I'd allowed him to get away.

"What happens now?" Zero took the seat next to me.

"You can get off home, but I'll need you to check the Premax tape in the morning. If you see anything out of the ordinary, give me a call."

"Okay, will do."

"And don't forget, I'm going to Roy's funeral tomorrow."

By five o'clock I was ravenous, and beginning to think that maybe Dale had checked out after all. The only ray of hope was that Lisa's phone was still in the hotel. At least, according to Zero it was.

I'd been in reception for so long that I'd attracted a few curious looks from the staff behind the reception desk. So far, thankfully, no one had challenged me.

I was seriously considering buying a fourth Mars bar when Dale came walking into reception. I was out of the chair like a flash, and I managed to get in the lift beside him.

"Which floor?" he said.

"Three, please."

"Same as me."

When the lift doors opened on the third floor, he did the gentlemanly thing, and stood aside so that I could get out first.

"Thank you, Mr Dale."

"Sorry, do I know you?"

"Could we speak in your room? Is Lisa in there?"

"Who are you?"

"My name is Kat Royle. I've been hired by your partner, Ted Fulton, to find you."

"I have nothing to say to you." He set off down the corridor towards his room.

"Mr Fulton is very worried about you."

"I've already told you. I have nothing to say."

"I guess I'll just let him know where you are, then."

"Do what you like. We're leaving."

"I've found you once. I can do it again. Wouldn't it be easier simply to talk to me?"

He stopped outside his door, and glared at me for the longest moment.

"You'd better come in."

"Mike, I was beginning to think —" The woman stopped mid-sentence when she saw me follow Dale into the room.

"You must be Lisa," I said.

"Who's she, Mike?"

"Fulton hired her to find me."

"Oh God!" Lisa slumped onto the bed. "Does he know where we are?"

Dale looked at me for an answer.

"Not yet."

"You can't tell him." She began to sob. "He'll kill Mike."

"Lisa!" Dale tried to close her down.

"She has to know, Mike. She has to know what will happen if she tells Fulton where we are."

"I need a drink." Dale walked over to the small desk, and picked up the half-full bottle of whisky. After pouring himself a shot, and downing it in one, he turned to us. "Anyone else want a drink?"

"I'll take one." Lisa wiped a tear from her eye.

I declined his offer.

"What did you say your name was?" Dale gave Lisa her drink, and then poured himself another one.

"Kat Royle."

"Well, Kat, you'd better grab a seat. This might take some time."

Chapter 20

Eighty percent of my wardrobe was black, which meant I didn't need to buy an outfit especially for Roy's funeral. It was scheduled for ten o'clock, so by lunchtime, it should all be over. I'd arranged to meet Sheila at the gates of St Augustine's church where the service was to be held.

I'd woken at just before six, and I hadn't been able to get off to sleep again. I hadn't heard from Zero, so I assumed the camera hadn't picked up any unusual activity overnight at Premax.

Toast and a cup of tea had been all I could face for breakfast. I was dressed and ready to go, but I still had almost an hour to kill before I needed to leave the flat. I considered walking to the church instead of taking a taxi, but I soon dismissed that idea when I glanced out of the window; the rain was coming down in buckets.

Just then, there was a knock at the door.

Please don't tell me Luke had cried off dog walking duties again. There was no way I could walk the dog, dressed like this, in the pouring rain. The Widow Manning would just have to do it herself this once.

It wasn't him.

"Graham? What are you doing here?"

"Nice to see you, too, Kat."

"I meant with the leg."

"I wasn't going to leave it at home."

"That was funny. For you."

"Thanks. I took a taxi."

"You should have phoned."

"I knew you'd tell me not to come over."

"You're right, I would have, but only because I'm going

to a funeral."

"Oh?"

"Can't you tell by the outfit?"

"You always wear black."

"Yeah, but I don't always wear sensible shoes and a skirt."

"That's true. I assume it's your boss's funeral?"

"Roy's, yeah."

"I won't keep you, but I wanted to explain about Sunday."

"There's no need."

"Yes, there is. I wanted to make sure you understood that Sharon and I are history. I had absolutely no idea she was coming over. I'm still not sure why she did. The only thing I can come up with is that she wanted to find out more about you."

"Why would she care? She was the one who dumped you, wasn't she?"

"It's just the way she is. Anyway, I wanted you to know that there's nothing going on between me and Sharon."

"Cool. So, now I know."

"I could come with you this morning if you like?"

That brought a smile to my face. "I don't think so."

"What's so funny?"

"Nothing. It's just that the first time we went out, you ended up at the hospital. Now, you want to top that by going to a funeral together. You sure know how to show a girl a good time."

"I thought you might appreciate the moral support."

"It's okay. I'm going with Sheila who used to work with me."

"Fair enough, but are you and I okay now?"

"Yeah, of course."

"So you'll go out with me again?"

"Are you really sure you want to? Look what happened to you the last time."

"I'm positive."

"Okay, but I'm not sure when it will be. I'm run off my feet at the moment."

"I'll give you a call." He leaned in, and was about to kiss me when my phone rang; Sheila's name popped up on caller ID.

"Sorry, I have to take this."

"Okay. Will you call me?"

I nodded.

"Soon?"

"Yes. Sorry, I really do have to answer this."

Back inside the flat, I took the call.

"Kat, it's me." She sounded as though she was crying.

"What's wrong?"

"I'm really sorry, but I'm not going to make it to the funeral. Don took a turn for the worse yesterday. The doctor reckons it's only a matter of days."

"I'm so sorry, Sheila. Is there anything I can do?"

"No, I'll be okay. I'm just sorry to let you down."

"Don't be silly. Your place is with Don now."

"Apologise to Anne for me, would you?"

"Of course, but she wouldn't expect you to be there under the circumstances."

"Okay. Thanks, Kat."

"Take care of yourself."

Poor Sheila. She and Don had been school sweethearts. I wasn't sure she'd ever bounce back from this.

I hadn't expected the church to be packed, but I had thought I'd find more than four people inside. One of them was the vicar.

Anne met me at the door. "Not a great turnout for him, is it, Kat?" She forced a smile. "Is Sheila coming?"

"She'd intended to, but her husband has only days to live. She sends her apologies."

"Poor thing. I had no idea. Has he been ill for long?"

"Yeah, months."

"The woman in the front pew is my Aunty Wynn." She gestured towards the diminutive figure.

"I didn't realise Roy had a sister."

"They fell out years ago. I'm surprised she turned up. I don't know the other two people, though."

"The old guy is the landlord of the Feathers—your dad's local. I spoke to him last week; his name's Lenny."

On the opposite side of the room, a little closer to the front, was a solitary woman who looked to be in her fifties. "I don't recognise the woman, though."

"Will you sit up the front with me, Kat?"

"Sure."

I seriously doubted that Roy had seen the inside of a church for the last three decades, so it came as no surprise that the vicar's eulogy bore little resemblance to the man I knew. A prayer and a single hymn later, we moved outside. This was the first burial I'd ever attended. The funerals I'd been to before had all been cremations.

Like an idiot, I hadn't thought to bring an umbrella, so as we made our way to the grave, I faced the prospect of getting soaked to the skin.

"Would you like to share this?" the solitary woman offered me shelter under her brolly.

"Thanks."

"I'm Sarah."

"Kat. I used to work with Roy."

"I think he mentioned you."

"Oh? How did you know Roy?"

"He was a friend. Do you know a man called Ray West?"

"Westy? Yeah, kind of."

"He and I were an item for a while, but then things turned nasty. Westy could be violent, and I was scared of what he might do to me. Roy let me stay at his place for a while. I hadn't intended coming today because I thought Ray might be here, but then I heard he'd died too."

The vicar said a few words before Roy's coffin was lowered into the ground. Anne wept, Roy's sister looked on impassively. Lenny checked his watch.

Afterwards, I said my goodbyes to Anne, and then hurried to catch up with Sarah who was headed towards the gates.

"Sarah! Hold on a minute."

"Sorry, Kat. I didn't wait for you because I thought you were staying with Roy's daughter."

"I've been trying to find out where Westy lived. I don't suppose you'd have any idea, would you?"

"It's over twelve months since I saw him, but the last I heard, he was staying with Tommy Hargreaves in Barking."

"You don't happen to have an address, do you?"

"Sorry. No."

***

I took a taxi back to the flat, and en-route, gave Zero a call.

"Hey, Kat."

"Where are you?"

"At the office. How was the funeral?"

"Depressing, but I may have got a lead on Westy. Can you see if you can track down someone called Tommy Hargreaves? He lives in Barking, apparently."

"Will do."

"I didn't hear from you this morning, so I take it nothing happened at Premax?"

"Nada. What's happening with the Dale case?"

"I'm going home to get changed, and then I'll come to the office. I'll update you then."

"Okay."

Back at my flat, I swapped the skirt and sensible shoes for jeans and trainers. By now, I was starving, so I grabbed a sausage roll from Greggs, and then headed for the tube station. I was just about to go underground when my phone rang; it was Zero.

"Got him," he yelled. "I've found Tommy Hargreaves."

"Already? That was quick. How did you manage it? More hacking?"

"He's in the phone book."

"Oh? Right."

Zero gave me the address in Barking.

"I might as well go there first before I come to the

office."

"What do you want me to do in the meantime?"

"Sit tight until I get in."

"I could be setting up the accounts."

"I thought you couldn't do that without the books?"

"It's not ideal, but if the books have gone for good, then I may as well do the best I can. If they do turn up later, I can always make the necessary adjustments."

"Okay, go for it. I'll see you later."

***

The man who answered the door had a small head in his hand.

"Mr Hargreaves?"

"Yeah?" He must have seen my confused look. "This is Jerry's head."

"Right." Like that explained it.

"Jerry's my puppet. I'm a ventriloquist."

"I see. I was told that Ray West lived here."

"Oh dear. Are you a relative of his? Or a friend? I'm sorry to have to tell you this, but he's dead."

"No, yeah, I know. I'm not a relative. We worked together. Sarah, his ex, gave me your address. She said that West—err—Ray had been living here."

"He said he only wanted to stay for a couple of weeks, but he was here for almost three months. I was going to have a word with him about moving out, but then he went and got himself murdered. I've still got a roomful of his rubbish."

"Oh? I don't suppose I could take a look at it, could I? He did some work for my company, and I think he still has some of my files."

"I don't see why not. There's nothing of any value as far as I can make out." He hesitated, suddenly a little self-conscious about what he'd just said. "I was only looking through it. I haven't taken anything."

"I understand. So, if I could maybe take a look?"

"Come in." He led the way upstairs to a small bedroom at the rear of the property. "It's a bit of a mess, but that's just how he left it."

"That's okay. You can leave me to it if you have stuff you need to do."

"I was just about to oil Jerry's head."

"Okay, then. I'll come down when I've finished."

If I'd known what I was letting myself in for, I'd have worn coveralls and a face mask. The smelly room was a disgusting mess with piles of unwashed clothes scattered all around. The drawers in the bedside cabinet were full of cigarette packets, some full, some empty. I found three pairs of glasses, an electric razor and a mobile phone the size of a brick.

But so far, no files.

Half an hour later, and I'd drawn a blank. The only place I hadn't checked was underneath the bed, and that was because I was worried about what I might find there. If the smell was anything to go by, it wouldn't be good. But I had no choice, so I took a deep breath and crouched down to get a good look. The source of the smell soon became apparent: there was all manner of half-eaten takeaways under there.

Gross!

I was about to beat a hasty retreat when I spotted a

small pile of folders at the far side of the bed, next to the wall. If I wanted them, and I did, I had no choice but to crawl under there.

Being ultra-careful to steer well clear of rotting food, I edged my way under the bed. Once I'd managed to grab the files, I reversed out of there as quickly as I could.

Bingo! A quick flick through revealed them to be related to cases that Westy had been working on for Roy.

Hargreaves now had a small leg in his hand. "Did you find what you were looking for?"

"Yes, thanks." I held up the files. "Is it okay if I take these?"

"No problem. Less for me to throw away."

"Thanks."

"Do you like ventriloquists?"

"I—err—"

"I could give you a sample of my act if you like. It'll only take me a minute to put Jerry back together."

"Thanks, but I really do have to get going. Maybe another time."

***

When I eventually made it back to the office, Zero had company.

"I hope you aren't corrupting my staff, Sonya," I said.

"Who? Me?" She grinned. "I was just showing him our latest catalogue. Wasn't I, Z?"

"Err, yeah." Zero's face was beetroot red.

"Sorry, Sonya." I thought I'd better come to his rescue. "We've got a ton of stuff we have to get through."

"It's okay. I should have been back from my ciggy break ten minutes ago. This young man of yours just wouldn't let me go." She blew him a kiss, and then made her exit.

"That woman's crazy," Zero said, once he was sure she'd gone.

"Are you going to take Sonya's catalogue home to show Toyah?"

"She'd kill me if I did." He threw it into the bin, and then gestured to the pile of files I had under my arm. "I take it you found Hargreaves?"

"Yeah. Westy had left these at his place for safekeeping. I've only had a quick glance through them while I was on the tube, but it looks like he worked on at least a dozen cases last year."

"Do you reckon you'll find whoever killed Roy and Westy in one of those?"

"I'd bet my life on it."

"I've set up the accounts as far as I can. If and when the books turn up, I'll have to add those details."

"What if they never turn up?"

"We'll just have to improvise."

"Right. Make us both a coffee, and I'll bring you up to speed on the Mike Dale case."

Chapter 21

I took a sip of the coffee. "You're getting better at making this, Zero."

"Thanks. Did you see Dale at the hotel?"

"I did more than that. I spoke to him, and Lisa. They're both very scared."

"Of what?"

"Ted Fulton. It seems that our client wasn't satisfied with the money he was making from the more conventional financial services, so he moved into what you might call *greyer* areas."

"Doing what?"

"If Dale is to be believed, money laundering. For some very nasty people."

"And you believe him?"

"I think so. If he's a liar, he's an incredibly good one. And besides, I don't believe Dale and Lisa could have faked the fear they showed when they thought I was going to give them up."

"But if Dale is a partner in the business, he must have known what was going on."

"He insists that he had no idea until he happened across some accounts he'd never seen before. When he confronted his partner, Fulton denied it at first, but when Dale wouldn't let it go, Fulton suggested he'd better drop it if he valued his health. That was the day that Dale made the decision to disappear."

"Why did Fulton come to you? He must have known there was a possibility you could find out about the money laundering."

"His own efforts to find Dale had drawn a blank. He

needed to find him, and just as importantly, he had to get his hands on that laptop. I'm convinced Fulton was behind the break-in at Dale's house. He must have paid someone to try and recover the computer. When that failed, he contacted our agency. Fulton simply couldn't afford to leave Dale out there because he was a loose cannon who could have brought his business crashing down at any moment—sending him to jail in the process. He no doubt gave instructions that Roy should simply find Dale, but not make contact with him. And, to be honest, if Roy had still been here, he would have done precisely that. He'd have pulled me off the case the moment I'd located the target. Roy was only interested in getting paid. He would have had absolutely no interest in why Dale had chosen to disappear."

"What do you think would have happened once Fulton knew where Dale was?"

"Your guess is as good as mine. Nothing good, I'm betting."

"What happens now?"

"I'm going to pay our Mr Fulton a visit. I'll give him enough rope, and see if he hangs himself."

"What do you want me to do?"

"I need you to go back to the hotel. Dale is expecting you."

"I'm not sure I'll make much of a bodyguard."

Zero was right; he would have struggled to fight his way out of a wet paper bag.

"That's not why I want you there. When Dale left work on that Friday evening, he intended to take what he knew to the police. That's why he took the laptop home with him. The problem is that the files are all password-protected, and Fulton must have changed it. That's what Dale has been doing since he went missing—trying to crack the password. Without any success, needless to say."

"And you want me to try to crack the password?"

"That's kind of what you do, isn't it?"

"Yeah, but what happens when I do crack it?"

"Dale will take what he knows to the police."

"But if you turn on Fulton, doesn't that mean we won't get paid?"

"Not by Fulton that's for sure. But Dale has said that if we help to put Fulton behind bars, he'll pick up our bill."

"Great. What are we going to do about Westy's files?"

"Once we've put the Dale case to bed, we'll need to work our way through those. I'm convinced our killer is somewhere in there."

***

After Zero had left, and before I set off for my little chat with Fulton, I gave Sheila a call, but it wasn't Sheila who answered the phone.

"Is Sheila there, please?"

"Who's calling?"

"Kat Royle. We used to work together."

"I'm afraid she isn't able to come to the phone at the moment."

"Is it Don? How is he?"

"I'm afraid Donald died in the early hours of this morning. I'm his sister, Flora."

"I'm so very sorry. Would you pass on my condolences to Sheila, and tell her I'm here if she needs anything?"

"Of course. Thank you for calling."

***

When I called Ted Fulton he demanded to know if I'd traced Dale. I told him I hadn't, but that I had some promising leads, and would need a little more information from him before I could pursue them further. He agreed I could go over to see him straight away.

I'd just left my flat when my phone rang.

"Kat, it's Christine."

"Hey. How are things?"

"Couldn't be better."

"That's good to hear. What happened with Ralph?"

"I decided to tell him everything."

"When you say *everything*?"

"I mean everything. I figured if we're going to make this relationship work, we both had to start being completely honest with one another. I told him that I'd thought he was having an affair, that I'd hired you to follow him, and that I knew about Fiona."

"Wow! I wasn't expecting you to do that. How did he react?"

"He broke down and cried. I think he was relieved that he didn't have to lie to me any longer. He tried to apologise for going to see Fiona, but I told him there was no need. And that I wished he'd felt he could discuss it with me before now."

"What did he say about my involvement?"

"That he'd always known you were a spiteful bitch." She laughed. "No, seriously, he was grateful that you'd told me everything because he wasn't sure he would ever have had the courage to do it himself."

"I'm so pleased for you. Both of you."

"Now that I don't have to hide any of this from him, I've put a cheque in the post to you rather than paying by cash. I hope that's okay."

"That's fine. Thanks."

"Can we get together for a coffee from time to time, Kat? I'd hate for us to lose touch again."

"Sure, I'd like that."

**

I was shown straight to Fulton's office.

"What's going on, Kat?" he demanded. "I was hoping for a result by now."

"Like I said on the phone, there are a couple of things I need you to clear up for me."

"What do you want to know?"

"When I took a look around Mike Dale's office, his laptop was missing."

"What about it?" he snapped. "It's in for repair."

"There's the strange thing. Your I.T. department have no record of taking it in for repair."

"Those geeks don't know what day it is most of the time."

"Maybe, but I managed to get a look at CCTV footage of this building taken on the day that Mike Dale disappeared."

"We don't have CCTV."

"True, but the bar across the road does. Fortunately, it caught Mike Dale as he left the building."

"So? How does that help?"

"He had his laptop with him."

"Oh?" Fulton seemed momentarily caught off guard, but quickly recovered. "What does that matter? I just need you to find him."

"I find it strange, that's all. Tasmin said that he never took his laptop home with him. Don't you find it curious that he should choose to do so on that day? It's almost as though he knew he wouldn't be coming back."

"I think you're reading far too much into it."

"Maybe. Tell me again, Ted, what exactly is it you do here?"

"We're financial consultants."

"Hmm? That could cover a multitude of sins, I'm guessing."

"I've heard enough." Red-faced, he stood up. "It's obvious to me that you're no nearer to finding Mike than last time you were in these offices."

"Maybe he doesn't want to be found? Have you ever considered that?"

"You're off the case. I'd like you to leave now or I'll have security show you out."

"No need. I'm going."

Once I was out of the building, I made a call.

"How's it going, Zero?"

"I'm working on it. It might take a while. How did you get on with Fulton?"

"He's kicked us off the case."

"That wasn't very nice of him."

"When I suggested he might be involved in some dodgy dealing, he turned a bright shade of red. A bit like you when Sonya's around."

"Don't remind me of that woman."

"Are they treating you alright over there?"

"Yeah, brilliantly. They've said I can order whatever I like from room service."

"That was nice of them. Look, I'm going to go back to the office and start working through Westy's files. Give me a call if you crack the password."

"Will do."

***

When I arrived at the Sidings, there was someone waiting for me outside my office. The man had sideburns. Very bushy sideburns.

As I approached him, he slipped his hand into his jacket pocket. If he had a knife, I was confident I'd be able to kick it from his grip before he had the chance to move towards me. But what if it was a gun?

It was neither.

"Kat Royle?" He produced a small brown paper packet.

"Who are you? And why have you been asking about me?"

"I'm Wesley Armitage."

"What do you want?"

"Just to give you this." He held out the package.

"What is it?" I took it from him, and to my surprise, found it was full of cash.

"It's all there. You can count it if you like."

"I think we should go into the office." I unlocked the door and led the way inside. "Take a seat, Mr Armitage. I think you'd better start by telling me what this money is for."

"It's for the work you did for me."

"I don't know you."

"Not you personally. Your agency."

"I've never seen you in the office."

"This is the first time I've been here. I was put in contact with Roy King through a friend of a friend. I always met with him in a pub."

"What was the case Roy worked on for you?"

"Actually, it wasn't Roy who worked on it. Someone called Westy handled it. My wife had been cheating on me with a man she worked with. Westy got photos of them together."

"When was this?"

"A couple of weeks ago. Roy said the payment had to be in cash, and that if I was late, Westy would pay me a visit. I tried to get hold of Roy to make the payment, but I couldn't reach him. Then, I heard that he'd been murdered, and found out that you'd taken over the business. I've been trying to find you since then to give you the cash. I don't want any trouble from Westy. He scares me."

"I can assure you that you have nothing to fear from him."

"That's a relief. Do you want to check that the cash is all there?"

"You have an honest face, Mr Armitage. I don't think that will be necessary."

"Thanks. So, you're sure about Westy?"

"Absolutely. You have my word on it."

When Armitage had left, I did count the money. All

eleven-hundred pounds of it.

That's what I called a result!

Now that I knew who the mysterious man with bushy sideburns was, I could discount him as the murderer, and instead focus on the cases that Westy had been working on. I was convinced that they would lead us to the killer.

***

By four o'clock, I'd finished going through Westy's cases. One of them had been for my new friend with the bushy sideburns. I'd ended up with a list of three possible candidates. Two of them, I already knew because we'd done work for them previously. The other man, I'd never heard of before, but judging by the nature of the case, he seemed worth checking out. I planned to pay each of them a visit over the next day or so.

I was almost out of the door when Zero called.

"I've cracked it, Kat!"

"That was quick."

"Are you kidding? I can't believe it took me this long."

"What's Dale doing now?"

"He said he's going to take a look through the files tonight, and then he and Lisa will go to the police first thing in the morning."

"Ask him if he wants me to go with him, would you?"

I waited until he came back on the line.

"He says they'll be okay."

"Fair enough. You might as well get off home, then. I was just about to leave myself."

"Did you go through Westy's files?"

"I did, and I've come up with a few people I plan to talk

to."

"Won't that be dangerous?"

"No more dangerous than waiting for them to find me. Oh, and by the way, we received a payment today. I've put it in your drawer. You'll need to enter it into your new accounts thingy."

"What was that for?"

"Payment for one of the cases Westy had been working on. It seems Roy was doing a lot of cash-in-hand work I knew nothing about."

"Okay, cool. I'll see you tomorrow."

Chapter 22

It had just turned six in the morning when I got the phone call. A whole hour before I had intended crawling out of bed.

"Kat, it's me."

"Zero? What's up?"

"It's Premax. I've just checked the overnight footage, and I think you'll want to see this."

"What happened?"

"A few minutes after the cleaners arrived, someone passed a dozen small boxes through the door. I couldn't see who they passed them to because we only have the one camera inside the loading bay."

"That's okay. I'm pretty sure I know who's on the other side of that door. I only have a link to the live feed. How can I get a look at that footage?"

"Check your email. I've already sent you another link."

"Okay. Hang on."

Moments later, I was watching the incident that he'd just described.

Bingo!

"That's fantastic, Zero!"

"What are you going to do now?"

"*We* are going to Premax. I'll call Kevin Lockhart at eight to see if I can set up a meeting sometime today. Sit tight there until you hear from me."

"Okay."

Fortunately, Lockhart was in the office when I called, and he was very keen to hear what I'd discovered. We arranged to meet at his offices at ten o'clock.

I got back to Zero and told him I'd meet him outside Premax, then after I'd showered and dressed, I took a leisurely walk to Geordie's. After the unexpected windfall from Mr Armitage, I figured the least I could do was to treat myself to a proper breakfast.

"Morning, Kat." Larry had his head buried in the local paper, the Lewford Chronicle. "Have you seen this?" He handed it to me.

The article, which had had Larry so engrossed, related to a local man who'd discovered he had a winning lottery ticket worth fifteen million pounds. According to the piece, the ticket had been in his fishing tackle bag, and would have expired in another two weeks' time.

"Fifteen million?" I started to daydream about what I could do with that kind of money. "Lucky sod."

"He doesn't deserve it if you ask me. I can't be doing with these people who buy tickets but can't be bothered to check them. If it were up to me, there'd be a seven-day limit for claiming prizes."

"What if you're away on holiday? Or in hospital?"

"Okay, two weeks, but no more." Larry was clearly prepared to countenance no further compromise. "What can I get you, Kat?"

"I'll have one of your small breakfasts, please."

Just then, my phone rang; Caller ID showed it was Bruce Layne.

"I'll bring it over to you, Kat," Larry said.

"Batman, have you got something for me?"

"The car that tried to run you over was stolen."

"Is that it?"

"Patience was never your strong suit, was it, Kat?"

"Sorry."

"We have footage of the driver when he abandoned the vehicle near the old docks."

"Any idea who it is?"

"None."

"Can't you run it through your face recognition software?"

"You've been watching too many movies." He laughed. "We don't have that yet. Certainly not for routine offences."

"*Routine*? Someone tried to kill me."

"The best I can do is to make sure all the local lads take a look at his face. One of them might recognise him."

"Can I get a look at it?"

"I'm not even supposed to be working on this."

"Come on, Bruce. No one need ever know."

The line went silent for the longest moment, and I was beginning to think he'd hung up.

"Okay. I'll text you the photo, but it'll have to be later today. I was due in a meeting five minutes ago. And remember, you didn't get it from me."

"You're a star, Batman."

"Yeah, yeah. And you owe me a pint. Several, in fact."

***

Punctual as always, Zero was waiting for me outside the gates of Premax. He was wearing jeans and a short sleeve t-shirt.

"Aren't you freezing?"

"Nah." He shrugged. "I don't feel the cold much."

"Clearly." I could see my breath, and I'd just been

thinking that I should have worn a jumper underneath my padded jacket.

Lockhart had us sent straight up to his office.

"Morning, Kat. Morning, err —"

"Zero."

"Sorry, of course. Take a seat."

We dispensed with the small talk, and got straight down to business. Zero brought up the previous night's footage on Lockhart's laptop.

"That's Desmond," he said, as soon as he saw the figure who was passing the boxes through the door. "He's in charge of security."

"That's a bit ironic."

"I don't understand." Lockhart sat back in his chair. "After you called earlier, I checked the overnight footage, but I didn't see any of this."

"Who's responsible in-house for your CCTV?"

Lockhart nodded as the realisation slowly sank in. "Desmond."

"Exactly. He doctored the CCTV."

"But how did you know?"

"We worked it out by studying the footage from the night of the previous theft."

"How did you manage to get hold of that?"

"That isn't important. We realised someone had edited it to remove a small section of footage. Just long enough to cover the couple of minutes it took to hand those boxes through the door."

"But I've checked that footage myself a dozen times. The timestamp doesn't show any editing."

"Whoever did this, knew what they were doing," Zero

chimed in. "They must have realised that if the timer jumped, they'd soon be caught. That's why they doctored the recording in such a way that the timer didn't show the edit."

"Then, how did you work out that a section had been removed?"

"We have a spider to thank for that," I said.

"Huh?"

After I'd explained to Lockhart how the 'jumping' spider had alerted Zero to the doctored footage, he asked, "How are they getting the speakers out of the gates? Do you have footage from outside the loading bay too?"

"No, but I'm almost certain I know how they're doing it. When I was working undercover with the cleaning crew, I came in on the minibus. I was the last one to be picked up, so I always ended up sitting on the back row of seats. No one wanted to sit there because there was less headroom. I didn't give it much thought at the time, but once I realised the thefts were taking place immediately after the cleaners had arrived, it was obvious that the only way they could have got those speakers out of the gates was on that minibus. I took a look at the same model of minibus recently, and the back seats are on the same level as the others. Someone must have modified the cleaners' bus to provide a small storage area where they could hide the speakers."

"Which must mean the driver is working with Desmond."

"That would be my guess."

Lockhart sat back in his chair, and was silent for a long minute. "It makes sense. Even if the guard on the gate checked the minibus, they wouldn't be looking for hidden storage areas."

"When I was on the minibus, the only thing they ever checked was our security tags."

"I still can't believe it's Desmond. He's been with me for twenty years."

"What are you going to do?"

"I'm going to sack his backside, and then I'm going to get the police involved. Twenty years or no twenty years, that doesn't give him the right to steal from me." Lockhart stood up. "I'm really grateful. To both of you. I must admit, I thought you were out of your depth at one stage."

"It's been a difficult time, what with Roy and everything."

"I'm sure it has. You'll let me have your bill, I assume?"

"You can rely on it."

***

Zero set off back to the Sidings while I headed for central London.

Malcolm "Malky" Moore had been a regular customer of RK Investigations for as long as I'd worked there. I'd never cared for the guy because there was something of the night about him. More importantly, I didn't approve of his business. Fortunately, I'd never been asked to work on any of his cases. He was a loan shark, but one who specialised not in making personal loans, but in loans to small businesses which couldn't raise cash through more conventional channels. What made it worse was that a lot of the businesses to whom he made loans were themselves rather dodgy. As you'd expect, his interest rates were obscenely high, but then he did expect to get stiffed more than the average bank. Malky often hired Roy to track down delinquent payers. Roy, in turn, often passed those cases onto Westy. Roy rarely discussed this kind of case with me, but he had on several occasions referred to Malky as a psychopath, and I was aware that the man had spent several stretches inside for violent crimes.

All of which begged the question: why was I on my way to see him?

Malky had a small office above a shoe shop near Seven Dials, but there was no sign to indicate the business was located there. I'd been there just once before when Roy had asked me to drop off some paperwork.

I pressed the intercom buzzer.

"What?" A female voice growled.

"I'd like to see Malky."

"Who are you?"

"Kat Royle."

"Never heard of you."

"I used to work for Roy King."

"Hold on."

I heard nothing else for several minutes, and I was about to buzz again when the door popped open.

The woman behind the desk obviously shopped at Mutton and Lamb.

"Malky says you're to go through." She stopped filing her nails just long enough to point to the door behind her.

"Thanks."

"Well, well, if it isn't young Kathleen. I heard about that boss of yours. Terrible business. Are you looking for a new job? I could always use a looker like you."

It made my skin crawl just to be in the same postcode as this man.

"Thanks, but I've taken over the agency. And the name's Kat."

"Come to see if I've got any work for you, have you? I'm sure we could come to some kind of arrangement."

"Actually, no." No matter how badly the business was doing, I was determined that I'd never work for the likes of Malky Moore. "I wanted to talk to you about some of the recent cases that Roy worked on for you."

"What about them?"

"It doesn't appear we ever received your payment for them. There are five, by my reckoning."

"You've got a damn cheek!" So much for Mr Nice Guy.

"Are you saying you did pay?"

"Why would I pay? Roy and that pal of his, Westy, were ripping me off."

"Ripping you off how? What were they doing?"

"They tried to tell me they'd been unable to collect the debts for at least half a dozen accounts, but they were lying. They got the cash and pocketed it themselves. Then they had the brass neck to try and collect their fees from me. Do I look stupid?"

I assumed the question was rhetorical. "How do you know they collected the money?"

"Because I wasn't born yesterday."

"You've heard that Westy was murdered too, I assume?"

"Course I did. Good riddance to the two of them as far as I'm concerned." He grinned. "Now I get it. That's why you're here. You think I offed them, don't you? You've got some balls, Kat, I'll give you that."

"Did you kill them?"

"What would you do if I said I had?"

It was a good question.

"My partner knows I'm here. If I don't check in within the hour, he has orders to contact the police."

"You're a terrible liar." Malky stood up and walked over to where I was standing; his breath was even worse than his dress sense. "No, I didn't kill them. Do you think I'd risk all of this for those two wasters? So, Kat, what do you say? How about we do some sweet business together?"

"Sorry, I've already got more work than I can handle." I began to backpedal towards the door.

"Pity. Still, if you change your mind, you know where you can find me."

"Right."

Back outside, the encounter had left me feeling like I needed to take a shower. Had Malky been right about Roy and Westy? Had they really collected Malky's cash, and kept it for themselves? I couldn't convince myself Roy would have done that. He would have been too afraid of the consequences. Westy, though? I wasn't so sure. That man had been a total headcase capable of anything.

Chapter 23

While I was on my way back to the office, my phone pinged with a text message. It was from Batman, and read: You owe me at least five pints.

Attached, was an image lifted from CCTV footage, and even though it was quite blurred, I recognised the man's face immediately.

"Batman, it's me."

"Jeez, Kat, I've already sent you the photo. Check your texts."

"I know. I've just seen it, thanks. That's why I'm calling. I know who he is."

"You do? Who?"

***

Back at the office, Zero was beavering away on the computer.

"Someone's busy," I sat on his desk. "Not too busy to make me a coffee, I hope?"

"Why didn't you tell me you'd found the books, Kat?"

"What are you talking about?"

"The accounts. You never said that you'd found them."

"That would be because I haven't. I definitely need a coffee because you're making even less sense than usual."

"They were on my desk when I got here. That's what I'm doing now. I'm trying to cross reference them with the case files, and entering them into the new accounts software."

"Whoa there! Back up a minute. You're saying that the books were on your desk when you arrived?"

"Yeah."

"Was the door unlocked?"

"No. I had to unlock it."

"So who put them there, and how did they get into the office?"

He shrugged. "I assumed it was you, and that you'd forgotten to mention it when I saw you earlier."

"Make that coffee, and bring it through to my office, would you?"

While Zero was making a drink, I received a phone call from Mike Dale. It was brief and to the point.

"That was Dale." I took a much needed sip of coffee. "He's just left the police station."

"What happened?"

"Not much yet, but he sounds a lot brighter. Relief, I guess. They're sending someone to question Fulton, and the chances are he'll be arrested. If not today, then soon. Dale expects to be arrested too, sooner or later."

"Why?"

"He was a partner in the business when the money laundering was taking place."

"But he didn't know about it."

"That's no excuse. He should have done. But the fact that he came forward as soon as he found out, and handed over the evidence, should go in his favour."

"Do you think he knew he'd be charged too?"

"I'm sure he did. He was more concerned about the threat from Fulton and the people behind him. Now that this is all out in the open, they aren't likely to do anything stupid."

"Is that it, then? Case closed?"

"For now it is, but I'm pretty sure the police will want to talk to me at some stage, to discuss our involvement."

"Does that mean I can raise a bill?"

"Yeah. Dale said to send it to his address in South Kensington. I'll let you have it."

"How did you get on with the loan shark guy?"

"Malky? I got out with all my limbs intact, so I'll chalk that up as a result."

"Do you reckon he's the one who murdered Roy and Westy, and who tried to bump you off?"

"He definitely wasn't the one who tried to run me over."

"How can you be so sure?"

"Because a friend of mine in the police force just sent me a photo of the man who was seen dumping the car that drove at me. It was a guy who I'd had a bit of a disagreement with earlier that day."

"What kind of disagreement?"

"He reckoned my half-dog had bitten his kid. He was going to hit the dog with a metal bar until I pointed out the error of his ways."

"What did you do? Did you deck him?"

"I prefer to think of it as disarming him with the minimum force necessary."

"And he tried to run you over for that?"

"Apparently. He clearly didn't take kindly to being humiliated by a woman. With a bit of luck, the police will be having a few words with him any time now."

"What about Malky, though? Do you reckon he might still be responsible for the two murders?"

"Let's just say he's a very strong candidate. He certainly has the motive. He's convinced that Roy and/or Westy were ripping him off."

"How?"

"He used RK Investigations to collect debts from small businesses who he'd given loans to."

"I thought we were private investigators, not debt collectors?"

"We are. At least, we are now. But Roy wasn't too particular about the type of jobs he took on. Anyway, Malky reckons that some of the money collected never found its way to him."

"How much money are we talking about?"

"I don't know."

"Enough for him to murder two people?"

"The amount isn't what's important. It's the principle. If word got out that Malky had allowed someone to cheat him, it would destroy his reputation. He might not kill for the money, but he would definitely do it to keep that reputation."

"Are you going to take this to the police?"

"It would be a waste of time, and besides, I don't know for sure yet that it was him. There are at least two other people I want to talk to first."

"Are they as bad as Malky?"

"One of them is worse. Much worse."

"Maybe you should take someone with you?"

"Are you volunteering?"

"I—err—"

"It's okay. I'm only joking. You've got your work cut out here with the accounts."

"Who do you reckon brought the books in, Kat?"

"I don't know, but whoever it was must have taken them from Roy because the last time I saw him alive was when he came to pick them up."

"Shouldn't you contact the police? Won't they want to dust the books for fingerprints or something?"

"It would be a waste of time. The police don't give a rat's arse about who killed Roy. The only way his murderer is going to be brought to justice is if I find him." I finished the last of the coffee. "And I'm not going to do that sitting here, chatting to you. I'm going to have a word with Rod "Masher" Masham."

"Who's he?"

"He's the guy I mentioned before."

"The one who's worse than Malky?"

"That's him. He came out of prison about a year ago."

"What was he inside for?"

"Murder."

"Are you going there now?"

"No time like the present."

"Are you sure you know what you're doing, Kat?"

"Probably not, but that's never stopped me before."

***

The address in the case file for Masher was a flat in Clapham Common. I'd never met the man in person, but I knew him by reputation. If the stories were to be believed, he'd run some kind of protection racket back in the nineties. That was before he was incarcerated for the murder of a rival who'd made the mistake of encroaching on Masher's patch.

Upon release from prison, and undeterred by his advancing age, he had apparently picked up where he'd left off in the protection business. Roy's involvement with this scumbag had been the surveillance of a number of individuals. The precise reason for the surveillance was unclear. Once again, it appeared that the majority of the grunt work had been carried out by Westy.

I'd been knocking on Masher's door for the last five minutes without any response.

"You're wasting your time there." A woman appeared at the door of the neighbouring flat.

"I'm looking for Rod Masham. Do you know where he is?"

"Down the crem, unless he's risen from the dead."

"He's dead?"

"He died last month. Had a heart attack in the Anchor."

"Are you sure?"

"Positive. I was in there when it happened. Best laugh I've had all year. Couldn't have happened to a nicer guy."

"Right. Thanks."

If what his neighbour had told me was correct, that would definitely rule Masher out of my enquiries because he'd died long before either Roy or Westy was murdered.

The final suspect was a man called Leroy Sanders, who was the only one of the three who didn't have a nickname. His case file was much thinner than the others, and gave no clue as to the nature of the work that Roy had undertaken on his behalf. I'd only included him in my list of suspects because of a cryptic note, in Roy's unmistakeable scrawl, that read: This guy is trouble.

Unfortunately, the case file contained no contact details for the mysterious Leroy Sanders, so I would have to get Zero to see if he could track him down.

***

On my way back to the office, I called in at McDonald's to grab a burger and fries. I really would have to improve my diet. Just not today.

"That was quick." Zero looked up from the computer.

"Rod Masham died of a heart attack before Roy and Westy were murdered."

"I guess that rules him out, then."

"Can you see if you can trace a guy called Leroy Sanders?"

"Sure. Kevin Lockhart called while you were out."

"Oh?"

"He confronted the security guy who denied everything at first. Until he saw our footage that is. Then he confessed. Lockhart has sacked him, and he has the police coming in to see him tomorrow."

"Brilliant. Don't forget you need to raise an invoice for that."

"Already done and in the post. Things are looking up."

"Except that now we have no paying cases on the books."

"That's the other thing I have to tell you. We had two calls while you were out. Potential new clients."

"Really?"

"Yeah. I've booked them in to come and see you tomorrow. I hope that's okay?"

"That's fantastic! How did they find me? Did you ask them?"

"Of course I did. They both found you on Facebook."

"Really? I knew social media would be good for the

business."

He grinned. "Who did?"

"Okay, you did. And to show my gratitude, I'll make us both a coffee."

"Do you even know how to?"

"Less of your cheek or I'll change my mind."

The phone rang again. It was an existing client who was checking if the agency was still open for business. Three in one day? Wow!

"How did you get on with the accounts?" I asked Zero over coffee.

"Okay, it's all done. There's something weird going on, though."

"Weird how?"

"Some of the cases aren't in the accounts at all."

"I already knew that. Roy was obviously working some cases on a cash-in-hand basis."

"That much is obvious. He was running two sets of accounts. The official ones for the cases that went through the books, and another set for the cash-in-hand jobs."

"So?"

"There are still some cases which don't appear in either set of accounts."

"How can that be? It doesn't make sense."

"Exactly."

After we'd finished our coffee, I told Zero he could call it a day and go home. I locked up and left thirty minutes later.

I was on my way out of the building when I bumped into Sonya.

"Hey, Kat. Where are you off to?"

"I've finished for the day."

"Nice work if you can get it. Is Sheila back at work, then?"

"Sheila? No, she's quit."

"I thought that was what you said, but I could have sworn I saw her earlier."

"Where? Here?"

"Yeah. She was headed down the stairs. She seemed in some kind of hurry."

"You must be mistaken. Her husband died yesterday. She'll be at home."

"I had no idea. Poor love. It must have been someone else I saw."

Chapter 24

The next morning, I felt like crap. Mainly because I'd woken at just before four o'clock, and no matter how hard I'd tried, I couldn't get back to sleep. My brain had decided to engage, and nothing I could do would disengage it.

The photo Batman had sent to me had taken me by surprise; I would never have believed that Charlie Beale would escalate something so ridiculously trivial in that way. On the other hand, it had come as something of a relief to know that whoever had murdered Roy and Westy wasn't also gunning for me.

I'd received a text from Anne the previous night, asking if I'd made any progress with finding her father's murderer. My response had been brief and guarded; I'd said simply that I was still working on the case, that I had nothing to report yet, but that I would let her know just as soon as I did. Malky Moore was still top of my list of suspects, but maybe that would change once I'd had a chance to speak to Leroy Sanders.

I was just on my way out of the flat when my phone rang.

"Kathleen?"

"Is everything okay, Mum?"

"Of course it is. I just wanted to know if you'd given any more thought to coming back home? Next Tuesday is the closing date to apply for those jobs at Lidl. Rachel Marsh has already been offered a position on the checkouts. You remember Rachel, don't you?"

"I don't think so."

"Yes, you do. Her mother has a limp."

"Oh yeah, the girl whose mother has a limp."

"You do remember her, then?"

"No. And anyway, I told you the last time we spoke. I've taken over the agency."

"I thought you might have changed your mind?"

"I haven't. In fact, things are going great. The new guy I've taken on, Zero, is doing really well."

"Hero?"

"Not Hero. It's Zero with a Z."

"What kind of name is that?"

"Look, Mum, I'm sorry, but I really do have to go. Maybe we could have a longer chat later in the week? One evening? I'll ring you."

"You'll forget."

"I won't. I promise. I have to dash now. Take care. Give my love to Jen."

On my way to the tube station, I gave Zero a call.

"Kat? I haven't had any joy tracing Leroy Sanders yet."

"That's okay. That's not why I called. I wanted to ask you what time those new clients are coming in."

"They're both coming in this afternoon: the first one at one-thirty and the next one at three."

"In that case, I'm going to shoot over to see Sheila this morning. I want to make sure she's alright."

"Okay. I'll see you later."

***

I'd only been to Sheila's house once before. That was over a year ago when Don had gone to stay with his brother for a long weekend.

I could have phoned ahead, but as she only lived twenty minutes away, I figured I had nothing to lose by dropping by on spec. I half-expected her sister-in-law to come to the door, but it was Sheila who greeted me.

"Morning, Kat. I've been expecting you."

"Oh? Right. I hope it's okay. I probably should have called first."

"Don't be silly. Come in, and I'll make us both a nice cup of tea."

"Why don't you let me do that?"

"Don't you start. I've had enough with Flora fussing around me."

"Where is your sister-in-law?"

"I sent her home. She was doing my head in."

We took our tea through to the living room where the first things I noticed were the framed photographs of Sheila and Don.

"I've been looking at those." She picked one up. "This one was taken at Southend. Don used to love Southend."

"He was a good-looking man. When was that?"

"The late seventies, I'd guess. Have a seat, Kat."

"You're looking better than I expected."

"I'm fine. At least, I will be once the funeral is out of the way."

"When is it?"

"A week tomorrow. At the crem. Will you come?"

"Of course I will. Is there anything I can do for you in the meantime? Anything you need?"

"No, thanks. Everything's pretty much in hand. Don insisted on making most of the arrangements himself, so there isn't much left for me to do. He was considerate like that."

"He was a good man. You were very lucky."

"It's about time you found someone yourself."

"Not you too." I smiled. "I've already got my mother on my case. She's trying to talk me into going back up north, getting a job at a supermarket, and settling down with a nice young man."

"Are you going to do that?"

"Not a chance. I love what I do, and I know this is a horrible thing to say, but I'm enjoying it even more now that Roy's gone."

"I half-expected you to call around last night."

"I'm sorry. I would have done, but I wasn't sure you'd be up to receiving visitors. I did speak to your sister-in-law on the phone."

"I meant after you'd found the books."

"*Books?*"

"I expected you to be in the office yesterday. When you weren't, I let myself in. I hope that's okay. I really should let you have the key back."

"Hang on. Are you saying it was you who left the accounts books in the office?"

"Yes, I would have waited there, but I didn't know how long it would be before you came back."

"But, I—err—" My head was spinning, as I tried to get to grips with what she'd just said. "Where did you get them?"

She sat back in the chair, and said nothing for the longest moment.

"I didn't intend to do it, Kat. I want you to know that."

"Do what? What are you talking about, Sheila?" Even as

I asked the question, I already knew the answer. But a part of me was praying that I was wrong.

"You know how Roy could be. You more than anyone. I tried to reason with him. I tried to explain why I'd done it, but he wouldn't listen. I begged him, Kat. I literally begged him, but he didn't hear. Or he didn't care."

"Sheila! I don't think you should be telling me this."

"I have to. That's why I left the books in the office. That's why I thought you'd come around last night."

"I — err — "

"I don't remember doing it. One minute he was shouting at me, and then the next minute, he was lying on the floor." She closed her eyes for a few seconds. "There was blood everywhere. I didn't know what to do."

"It's okay. Take a breather. I'll go and make us another drink."

As I waited for the kettle to boil, I tried to get my head around what Sheila had just told me. It wasn't easy.

"Thanks, Kat." She took the cup of tea from me. "Please don't hate me."

"Don't be daft. Of course I don't hate you."

"I only went around there to try and reason with him. I was in the wrong for taking the money, I knew I was, but like I said to him, I'd only done it for Don. I told Roy I'd make sure I paid him back. Every penny. It would just take a while."

"Is that why you didn't want him to take the books when he came into the office that day?"

"Yeah. He'd never shown any interest in the accounts, just as long as there was cash in the bank. But we'd been through a particularly bad period, and the cashflow had all but dried up. I knew if he got someone to take a look at the books, they'd soon work out what had happened."

"Why didn't you tell me you were having money problems?"

She smiled. "You never had two pennies to rub together, and besides, it wasn't your problem."

"I would have tried to help."

"I know you would. I honestly thought I'd be able to pay back the money before Roy noticed it was missing, but the bills kept piling up, and—well, you know the rest." She began to cry.

I walked over and gave her a hug. "It's going to be okay. I promise."

I held her for several minutes while she sobbed. Eventually, she said, "I need you to do me one favour, Kat."

"Of course. Anything. Just name it."

"I want to go to Don's funeral."

"Of course you do. What do you need? Cash? Is there something you want me to arrange?"

"Nothing like that. That's all taken care of. I just need you not to go to the police until after the funeral."

"I'm not going to tell them anything. Ever. They think it was a burglary. There's no need for them to—"

She raised a hand to silence me. "After the funeral, I'll hand myself in."

"You can't do that."

"I have to, Kat. I couldn't live with the guilt. Roy was a horrible man, but he didn't deserve to die. I'll hand myself in the day after Don's funeral. And of course, I won't mention this little conversation. No one need ever know that you knew what happened."

I spent the best part of an hour trying to talk Sheila out of giving herself up to the police, but she was adamant it was something she had to do.

"I'm sorry, Kat, but I'm feeling really tired now. I'd like to go and have a lie down."

"But, Sheila, please. Please don't—"

She stood up. "There's something I need to give to you before you go." She went to the sideboard, and took something out of the top drawer. "Give this to Anne after Don's funeral, would you?" It was the missing Rolex. "I only took it to make them think there had been a burglary. Tell her that I'm sorry, would you?"

***

I don't remember walking to the station or getting on the tube, but the next thing I knew, I was at the Sidings.

"Kat? Are you okay?" Zero was at his desk. "You look terrible."

"I'm fine."

"Is it your friend? Is she okay?"

"Err, yeah, she's alright."

"Do you want a coffee?"

"Yes, please. Make it stronger than usual, would you?"

"There you go." He joined me in my office. "Hot and very strong."

"Thanks." I took a sip.

"Are you sure you're okay?"

"Positive. You'd better brief me on the two new clients who are coming in this afternoon."

"Okay, but first, I've managed to track down Leroy

Sanders. I've got an address for him."

"I won't be needing that now."

"How come?"

"I just won't. Let's talk about the new clients."

Before we could, my phone rang.

"Kat, it's Bruce."

"Hey."

"I just wanted to let you know that your buddy, Charlie Beale, has been arrested. He'll probably be charged with dangerous driving."

"Right."

"Is that it? I thought you'd demand he was charged with attempted murder."

"What good would it do? Realistically, that's never going to happen, is it? Thanks for letting me know."

"Hold on. That's not all. I thought you might be interested to know that the Bell brothers, Alan and Kevin, have been arrested, and charged with the murder of Ray West. Apparently, Westy had been playing around with Alan's wife."

The Bell brothers were notorious thugs who ran an illegal betting operation out of a garage in Lewford. No one with even half a brain would cross them.

"Oh? Okay, thanks for letting me know."

"That's it? I thought you'd be —"

"Thanks, Bruce. Bye."

***

That evening, Graham phoned to ask if I wanted to go over to his place, but I fobbed him off with the excuse that I had a headache and needed a quiet night in. I'm pretty sure he knew I was giving him the brush-off, but I didn't care. All I could think about was Sheila.

When my phone rang, I was sure it would be Graham, trying to get me to change my mind.

"Kat, it's Pat."

"What's wrong? Is it Vi?"

"Yeah. I don't know what's happened, but there was a police car and an ambulance at her house."

"Is she okay?"

"I'm not sure. I asked the policeman, but he wouldn't tell me anything."

"Did you see her?"

"No, by the time I got out there, the ambulance had already gone."

"Do you know where they've taken her?"

"Not for sure, but I'd guess University Hospital."

"Okay, thanks. I'll get straight over there."

By the time I got downstairs, my Uber ride was waiting for me. The journey only took a few minutes, but it felt like a lifetime. If anything had happened to Vi, I'd hunt down the perp and kill him.

As my ride pulled into the drop-off point, I spotted a police car parked near the main entrance. Standing next to it was Constable Sharp.

"Where is she, Sharpy?"

"What are you doing here, Kat?"

"Looking for my grandmother. Is she okay?"

"She's fine."

"Where is she? I want to see her. What did that scumbag do to her?"

"She isn't here."

"Which hospital did they take her to?"

"She's not in hospital. She's down the station."

"What's she doing there?"

"Being questioned."

"About what?"

"Assault, I'd guess."

"You're not making any sense, Sharpy. Her neighbour told me there was an ambulance at her house."

"That was for the conman. From what I hear, your grandmother caught him going through her drawers, so she chased him out of the bedroom, and pushed him downstairs. He's got a broken leg and concussion."

Chapter 25

Nine months later

Sheila gave me a little wave from across the huge room. I never ceased to be amazed by just how bright she was whenever I visited her.

"Thanks for coming, Kat." She stood up and gave me a hug.

"How are you? You're looking well."

"I'm great. What about you?"

"Same old, same old."

Ramsford prison was a two-hour train journey from London. I tried to visit Sheila at least once a month, if I could. After pleading guilty to manslaughter, she'd been sentenced to eight years behind bars.

"How's that young man of yours, Kat?"

"Graham's just fine."

"Have you moved in together yet?"

"You asked me the same thing the last time I was here. The answer is still the same. No."

"Why not? What are you waiting for?"

"I'm perfectly happy with the current arrangement."

She gave me that look of hers. "What about Graham? How does he feel about it?"

"I've told him that he's happy with the current arrangement too."

"You never change. Just don't let him slip through your fingers. The good ones don't come along very often."

"I'll bear that in mind."

Her smile suddenly faded. "I had an unexpected visitor last week."

"Oh?"

"Anne came to see me. She sent in a request just after your last visit. She was the last person I thought would want to visit me."

"How did it go?"

"She was lovely. I'd been terrified about seeing her, but she seemed to go out of her way to put me at ease."

"What did she have to say?"

"Just that she didn't bear me any ill will." Sheila reached into her pocket for a tissue. "She said she'd forgiven me. It's much more than I deserve."

"Don't be silly. If Roy's daughter can forgive you, then the least you can do is forgive yourself."

"I'll try." She wiped away a tear. "Anyway, I want to hear all of your news. How's the business going?"

"Really well. We're run off our feet."

"You shouldn't be wasting your time coming to visit me, then."

"Don't be soft. I can always make time for that."

"Is that young man with the funny name still working for you?"

"Zero? Yeah, he's doing great. When I originally set him on, I thought he'd just be doing the admin stuff you used to do, but he's working on cases more or less full-time now. He's a natural. And when it comes to computers and stuff like that, he's a genius."

"That's fantastic. And there's enough work to keep the two of you busy?"

"Too much. I'm using a couple of other people on an as-needed sub-contract basis."

"I hope they're not like Westy."

"Nothing like him. They're both down-to-earth, honest guys. And you'll never guess who I've got working in the office now."

"I've no idea."

"Sonya."

"Sonya from the naughty shop?"

"The what?" I laughed. "Who calls it that?"

"I do. She tried to show me one of her catalogues once. I've never seen anything quite like it."

"She handed her notice in at BuyVrator a couple of weeks ago, and now she's working full-time in the office. Much to Zero's displeasure."

"Doesn't he like her?"

"She scares him. You know how she can be: larger than life and twice as brassy. He has absolutely no idea how to deal with her. She only has to say good morning to him and he blushes."

"Poor little love."

"He'll get used to her." I grinned. "Eventually."

***

On the train journey back into London, my phone rang.

"Hi, Grandma."

"Are you tired of breathing?"

"Sorry, Vi. How are you?"

"I'd be a lot better if a certain granddaughter of mine hadn't forgotten where I live."

"I was only over there last week."

"It was the week before."

"Sorry. It's just that I've been so busy."

"I still haven't met that boyfriend of yours. Why are you hiding him? Is he ugly or something?"

"I'll bring him over to see you the next time I come."

"You said that the last time, and the time before that."

"This time I definitely will. I promise."

"When?"

"How about next Wednesday?"

"Okay. Does he like corned beef hash?"

"I doubt he's ever had it, but I'm sure he'll love it."

"Okay. Next Wednesday it is, and don't come alone or I won't be best pleased."

"We'll both be there. I promise."

As soon as I was done with the call, I gave Graham a ring.

"Hey, City Boy, how's it hanging?"

"It'd be a lot better if I got to see you more often."

"It's funny you should say that. What are you doing next Wednesday evening?"

"Wednesday? Nothing, I don't think."

"In that case, you and I are going out for dinner."

"Not the Gerbil. Anywhere but the Gerbil."

"Do you like corned beef hash?"

"Do I like *what*?"

"That's what I thought you'd say. We've been invited for tea at my Grandma Vi's."

"Isn't she the one who threw that conman downstairs?"

"She didn't throw anyone down the stairs. Don't you recall that the police accepted her version of events? He tripped in his hurry to get away."

"Oh yeah." Graham laughed. "I also remember you telling me that he was lucky she hadn't battered his head in while he was lying at the bottom of the stairs."

"You'll love her, I promise."

"Okay, it's a date."

***

When I arrived at the Sidings, Zero was at his desk, muttering under his breath.

"What's up with you?"

"It's that stupid woman again."

"I assume you're talking about Sonya?"

"Who else? She does my head in."

"Where is she?"

"She's just nipped out to buy a sausage roll or twenty. Do you know what she left in the top drawer of my desk?"

"It wasn't another sex toy, was it? I had a word with her about that last week."

"No, it was this." He took out a small book titled: Fashion Tips for Nerds.

"Oh dear." I tried not to laugh, but I couldn't help myself. Zero was a real asset to the business, but his fashion sense left a lot to be desired.

"What's wrong with what I wear?"

"Nothing." I shook my head. "Much."

We went through to my office, and started to review the cases.

"Hello, anyone home?" The woman's voice came from the outer office.

"We're through here!"

It was only then that I spotted the look of horror on Zero's face.

"Mum?" he said. "What are you doing here?"

"I've been asking you to show me where you work for months, and it's obvious you're never going to, so I thought I'd come and see for myself." She turned to me. "I hope you don't mind, Ms Royle?"

"It's Kat, and of course I don't mind. Take a seat. Would you like tea or coffee?"

"A coffee would be nice."

"You heard the lady." I nodded to Zero. "Off you trot."

"I can't remember the last time Nero made me a drink," she said.

Nero?

Zero looked as though he wanted the ground to open up and swallow him.

"Why don't you leave your mum and me alone so we can have a little chat?" I said, once we had our drinks.

He didn't look thrilled at the idea, but he skulked out of the room anyway.

"I have to be honest with you, Kat, when Nero first told me he was coming to work for you, I was a little worried, but it's done him a power of good. He's so much happier, and much more confident now. Thank you for taking a chance on him."

"No thanks necessary, Mrs Smith."

"Call me Freda."

"He was taking a risk too, Freda. When he joined me, there was no guarantee the business was going to make it."

"But things are okay now, aren't they?"

"Definitely. We're going from strength to strength. And that's in no small part, due to your son."

"That's great to hear."

The two of us chatted for half-an-hour or so before Freda went on her way.

"So, *Nero*?" I grinned. "Is there anything you'd like to tell me?"

"Okay, I lied about my name. I hate it. Everyone calls me Zero."

"It's okay. You can call yourself whatever you like, just as long as you do your job."

"Do you promise never to call me Nero again?"

"Cross my heart."

"*She* might not," Sonya said through a mouthful of sausage roll. "But you can bet your bottom dollar that *I* will."

"If you do, I'll kill you!" Zero shot her a look.

"That's enough!" I thumped the desk. "You two have got to learn to work together or you'll have me to answer to."

"It's not me, it's her," Zero protested. "We were okay until she joined us."

"I said that's enough, Zero. You and I still need to run through the current cases. Sonya, have we had any new enquiries this morning?"

"Two." She swallowed the last of the sausage roll. "A guy reckons his neighbour is an alien. I filed that one in the nutter file."

"Right."

"The other one sounds more promising. The MD of a business called Reed Brothers called. His company manufactures some kind of component for mobile phones. He reckons one of his competitors is trying to steal his designs. I said you'd give him a call back later today."

"Great. And have you brought the accounts up to date?"

"I've made a start on them, but I might need the *emperor's* help."

"In that case, can I suggest you try to be nicer to him?

And you can start by calling him by his chosen name."

"But Kat, it's just a bit of fun."

"Sonya! Ask him nicely."

"Do I have to?"

"Unless you can manage to do the accounts all by yourself, then yes."

"Okay. Will you help me with the accounts, please?"

"Sorry, were you talking to me?" Zero shrugged.

"Will you help me with the accounts, please, *Zero*?"

"It will be my pleasure." He couldn't have looked any smugger if he'd tried.

Just then, a delivery man came through the door; he was red-faced and out of breath.

"You should get a lift in this place. Is this R.K. Investigations? I've got a parcel for Kat Royle."

ALSO BY ADELE ABBOTT

The Witch P.I. Mysteries
(A Candlefield/Washbridge Series)

Witch Is When... (Books #1 to #12)
Witch Is When It All Began
Witch Is When Life Got Complicated
Witch Is When Everything Went Crazy
Witch Is When Things Fell Apart
Witch Is When The Bubble Burst
Witch Is When The Penny Dropped
Witch Is When The Floodgates Opened
Witch Is When The Hammer Fell
Witch Is When My Heart Broke
Witch Is When I Said Goodbye
Witch Is When Stuff Got Serious
Witch Is When All Was Revealed

Witch Is Why... (Books #13 to #24)
Witch Is Why Time Stood Still
Witch is Why The Laughter Stopped
Witch is Why Another Door Opened
Witch is Why Two Became One
Witch is Why The Moon Disappeared
Witch is Why The Wolf Howled
Witch is Why The Music Stopped
Witch is Why A Pin Dropped
Witch is Why The Owl Returned
Witch is Why The Search Began
Witch is Why Promises Were Broken
Witch is Why It Was Over

Witch Is How... (Books #25 to #36)
Witch is How Things Had Changed
Witch is How Berries Tasted Good
Witch is How The Mirror Lied
Witch is How The Tables Turned
Witch is How The Drought Ended
Witch is How The Dice Fell
Witch is How The Biscuits Disappeared
Witch is How Dreams Became Reality
Witch is How Bells Were Saved
Witch is How To Fool Cats
Witch is How To Lose Big
Witch is How Life Changed Forever

Susan Hall Investigates
(A Candlefield/Washbridge Series)
Whoops! Our New Flatmate Is A Human.
Whoops! All The Money Went Missing.
Whoops! Someone Is On Our Case.
Whoops! We're In Big Trouble Now.

Web site: AdeleAbbott.com
Facebook: facebook.com/AdeleAbbottAuthor

Printed in Great Britain
by Amazon

82893609R00150